QUIZ

The War Between the Pitiful Teachers and the Splendid Kids

1. The leader of the kids was:
   a) Timmy Smith
   b) Timmy Roddy
   c) Skinny Malinky
   d) all of the above, sometimes

2. When the kids tried to catch the teachers in Shark-Infested Rice Pudding the teachers:
   a) ate all the pudding
   b) lectured the shark on the "aesthetic experience"
   c) mistook the shark for a visiting consultant
   d) all of the above

3. The teachers were afraid of Big Alice because:
   a) she was a hyena
   b) she was a kid
   c) she ate Mrs. Jerome
   d) all of the above

4. The kids never stood a chance against the teachers because Mr. Foreclosure:
   a) had a secret weapon
   b) commanded an army of educators
   c) was a poisonous red ant
   d) all of the above

5. Ultimately, the war was won when:
   a) Skinny escaped the Status Quo Solidifier
   b) Big Alice r
   c) the Bookw
   d) all of the a

`·p (5    ·p (4`

Other Avon Flare Books by
Stanley Kiesel

SKINNY MALINKY LEADS
THE WAR FOR KIDNESS

THE WAR BETWEEN THE PITIFUL TEACHERS AND THE SPLENDID KIDS

STANLEY KIESEL

AN AVON FLARE BOOK

Editor: Emile McLeod

AVON BOOKS
A division of
The Hearst Corporation
105 Madison Avenue
New York, New York 10016

The E.P. Dutton, Inc. edition contains the following Library of Congress
Cataloging in Publication Data:

Kiesel, Stanley
  The war between the pitiful teachers and the splendid kids.
  Summary: After years of persecution, schoolchildren led by Skinny Malinky
finally declare war on their teachers and the system they represent.
  [1. School stories. 2. Teacher-student relationships—Fiction] I. Title.
PZ7.K544War   1980   Fic   8-13450

First Avon Flare Printing: January 1982

Printed in the U.S.A.

K-R   19   18   17   16   15   14   13   12

Acknowledgment

The Sturdy and Sparkle sequence on page 20 has been paraphrased from "Sturdy and Sparkle," which appears in *3142 Lyndale Ave. So., Apt. 24 Prose Poems* by Keith Gunderson (Minnesota Writers Publishing House, 1975).

for Clyde Robert Bulla

Contents

PART TWO

PART ONE

1

Ida

It was after school, and the janitor expected to find this last classroom empty. She found a small, red-haired boy at the blackboard, pocketing a piece of chalk. "This your room?" she asked.

"Yes."

"That your chalk?"

"No."

"Give it, then. And skedaddle."

The boy couldn't have been more than five or six. There was a galaxy of freckles across his face, and his hair fell on his forehead like an orange, Hokusai wave. "I want it."

"Ask for it, then. That's the way." The chalk was handed over. She placed it on a table.

"Miss Nelson's got a boxful."

The large, black woman laid down her rag and studied the boy. "How come you so needful of chalk? What's your name?"

"Skinny. My name's Timmy, but everyone calls me Skinny."

A big laugh a kid could lie back and stretch in gushed out of the janitor. "Well, names don't lie. I expect Red ought to follow you about."

"Well, it doesn't. No one ever calls me Red. Do you clean this room every day?"

"When Jim don't. You know Jim?"

"I seen him but I don't know him. Can I have the chalk now?"

The woman turned her broad back, running her rag along the chalk tray. "No," she replied, and she heard the sharp crack of chalk being dashed to pieces on the floor. The boy was gone.

The next afternoon he was waiting in the same room.

"I'm not exactly happy at seein' *you* again," she said placing a bucket in the sink.

"I'm sorry I threw the chalk. It wasn't aimed at you."

"Don't matter where you aim, I got to clean it up."

"Can I fill?"

She stood aside, watching him as he turned the faucet. After a minute she said, "Better trot home. Your mama's gonna be wonderin'."

"I don't have a mama." He lifted the bucket with two hands and eased it down to the floor, slopping water on his shoes. Both pretended not to notice. He peered into the bucket. "Is that how much water?"

"I guess it's enough." She proceeded to dip a sponge into the water, wringing it out several times. "What you mean, no mama?"

"I live with my foster family, Mr. and Mrs. Atkin. And they have lots of foster babies around, so they don't notice how late I get home."

"Okay, Skinny." She handed him the sponge. "You can do one job for Ida. Wet down the board. Don't drip. When you have to, wet it in the bucket again. Squeeze out good."

Skinny happily did as he was told.

"How old are you?"

"Five and a half."

"You sure do need some meat on your bones."

"I don't eat much."

"Better squeeze one more time."

Skinny got into the habit of staying after school and keeping Ida company. She put him to work.

One day, Ida paused before the blackboard and pointed to where the teacher had printed PLEASE SAVE beside a list of names. "How come, Skinny, you always on that list?"

"'Cause I'm bad. That's the kids who do bad things."

"Like what?"

"Oh, throwing things. Like sand. Or knocking blocks down. Or pushing to be first in line. Or talking back."

"You talk back? That *is* bad. You gotta talk *front* first insteada *back.*"

"How do you talk front?"

"You look a person straight in his eye, hopin' for yes and ready for no. If no comes, you chew it up the best way you know how, 'cause someday you gonna pass that no to someone else. You want *that* person to respect your no. That what makes people get along. When you talk *back,* you just showing you can't take no. There's more no's than yes's around. Yesirree."

"Why can't I get all yes's, Ida?"

"'Cause that's not how the world's set up. That's why you so skinny. Hungry for yes's. Now you just follow me in here," and she pushed through the door to the lavatory.

Ida plunged a thick forearm into a toilet and scrubbed furiously. "See this arm? It hasn't said no to toilet for a long time. It say yes. It still knows how to talk front."

"Do you like that job, Ida?" And Skinny made a face. "I wouldn't like to clean toilets."

"Well, Skinny. Maybe you're going to have to one of these days. Cleanin' toilets is a little yes. Every day is made of little yes's. They give you practice so you can say the big yes when it comes."

"What's a big yes?'

"Oh, you'll know it when you find it." She looked down her bosom at a loose thread. "Uh-oh. Lost my button."

"Here it is," shouted Skinny, peering down the small drain hole in the floor.

Ida bent down, lifted the grate, and tried to force her hand into the drain.

"Here, let me do it!" Skinny wiggled his hand in and, after a minute, drew up a wet pearl button.

Ida grinned. "You a real Skinny Malinky all right."

The boy opened his eyes wide. "That's going to be my name," he said.

And it was. Skinny's last name had always been the name of the latest foster family he happened to be living with. The name Smith was in parentheses on all of Skinny's school records. That was because two Smiths had brought Skinny into the world. Then they gave up on him, and Skinny was found in a box of shopping bags in the hallway of a walk-up apartment when he was one week old. Someone who claimed to be his grandmother took care of him until he was two, and then she died, and Skinny was taken over by a state facility. The state facility gave him bed and board until he was five. Then Skinny began a round of foster homes. Now it was the Atkins' turn.

"Mrs. Atkin had to come to school today," Skinny said to Ida.

"How come?"

"Because I don't copper-ate."

"How'd it go?"

"Well, I had to leave the room, but I seen through the window how teacher showed all my need-to's to Mrs. Atkin."

"What're need-to's?"

"You know. Need-to copper-ate. Need-to put blocks away. Need-to raise your hand."

"Oh yeah. *Them* need-to's."

"Do you clean Room 4, too, Ida?"

"Yep. Why?"

"'Cause that's where I'm going next. I'm getting a new teacher. Miss Long in Room 4."

"Hmm. She a tough cookie, Miss Long. She always leaves me fussy notes." Ida shook her head and drew an arm over a perspiring forehead. "She some sort of captain and sure knows it."

"She's so-cial chairman."

"Is that it? She always bringing flowers to school. But, behind them flowers, she don't smile."

A few weeks passed before Ida saw Skinny again. He showed up one afternoon at four-thirty, as Ida was mopping down the floor of Room 7.

"What'sa matter, Skinny? Miss Long?"

Skinny's voice was thin and weary. "No. I got a new foster mother." He sighed. "Mrs. Laurel Roddy."

"See those books? Put 'em on that table. . . . What's she like?"

"She drinks a lot. She sleeps a lot, too."

Ida paused and tut-tutted. "How come they keep you there, then?"

"She gargles before the social worker comes. She has as many gargle bottles as wine bottles. Five. I counted them."

"But you still in this school?"

"Sure. I'm in the same neighborhood."

Ida stood and cuffed his wild, red hair. "Well, you come visit me long as you want."

For several months Skinny was a constant visitor. He teetered on chairs to close windows, he pushed chairs under tables, he filled the empty paper towel dispensers. Then the school year ended.

The following term Ida didn't see much of Skinny. He visited twice, helping Ida clean blackboards. He had grown taller, but he was still bony, and his freckles appeared darker and his hair more unruly.

"You still livin' with that gargle lady?" Ida asked him one day.

"Yeah. But I don't see her much."

"I seen a note on Miss Rumstead's desk about you." Silence. "It say 'requests a meetin'.' With your foster mama. It say *serious* and plenty a' big words. I know they gonna give you trouble."

"Mrs. Roddy don't read notes. She's usually out cold on the sofa."

"You're makin' big talk in the teachers' lunchroom, Skinny Malinky," Ida's eyes bore down on the boy. "You raisin' hell."

Skinny scowled and looked away. "See ya, Ida," and he dashed out onto the asphalt yard and vanished.

2

Ida's Research

Ida was tidying up Miss Rumstead's desk. She came across a folder across which was written: "Anecdotal Record of Timmy Roddy (Smith)—Skinny Malinky." She grunted and opened it. There were several pages clipped together. She pushed the clip off and held the first page close to her eyes.

October 20th   Monday
Refused to work on committee studying Alaskan Imports and Exports. Drew pictures instead. The pictures were all of teachers and quite scurrilous. I showed them to Miss Rucksnack, my supervisor, and she filed a report.

October 28th   Tuesday
Late again. Had no written excuse. Foster mother could not be contacted. During the spelling test, I discovered he had substituted his own words with accompanying definitions. Samples (I quote verbatim): "*clummy:* a wet smile attached to a teachers dry eyie. *enkwort*: a writing blister which happens to kids fingers when they touch words. *runchbag*: the wrong kind of sandwich for a kids lunch." And so on. I

explained to him that he had a responsibility to learn how to spell the words on our class list before experimenting with words on his own. He tore up his paper, threw the pieces at me, and sulked for the rest of the day.

October 29th   Wednesday

When the nurse visited today to give her puppet show about dental hygiene, I made sure Skinny was seated near me. Miss Hodges has developed a very nice presentation showing how to brush teeth correctly, but almost as soon as she began, Skinny interrupted, "Are the two puppets related?"

Miss Hodges handled it well. She replied, "Yes. They are brother and sister. Sturdy and Sparkle are their names."

But as she went on, Skinny insisted on breaking in with silly or sarcastic comments: "How come it's the boy who doesn't brush right?" "Why don't they do something else besides brush their teeth?" "I would rather brush my teeth fast every crazy which way."

Miss Hodges, unfortunately, asked, "Why?"

"Because if I brushed like Sturdy and Sparkle, I'd feel just like a puppet in a blue-and-white sailor suit with someone's hand inside my back and fingers up my arms, and I'd rather feel like a criminal than feel like that." The class erupted and poor Miss Hodges left, the puppets limp on her hands. I told her to file a report.

A few days later, Ida found yet another folder on Miss Rumstead's desk. This one was labeled: "Timmy Roddy (Smith)." She opened it to find only one paper. It was pink, and at the top was the title: Parent Conference Report—CONFIDENTIAL. Ida leaned her broom against a table, sat, and read the paper.

Mrs. Roddy, Timmy's foster mother, arrived thirty-five minutes late. I showed her Timmy's progress report and explained how Timmy was failing in all academic subjects. Recommended remedial classes. She said (I quote as clearly as I can remember): "Skinny got a good head, but you don't know about heads like his. Just because he different you don't expect much. He's not your background so you don't try hard." I replied that I wasn't sure what she meant by *background*. She just laughed. I tried to remain calm.

Timmy spends more school time *outside* class than *inside,* and he attracts a large number of other children to instigate unruly and improper acts of minor sabotage in the halls. I recommend a special training facility for Timmy.

Mrs. Roddy said she had an appointment and marched out of the room.

Ida replaced the paper in its folder. "Bad news!" she muttered.

During the next few years Ida saw very little of Skinny. One morning when she worked in the kindergarten yard sweeping up sand near the sandbox, he peered at her from outside the fence and waved, a notebook under his arm.

"Hi, Ida!"

"Hi, Skinny. C'mere!"

"Can't, Ida. Gotta go somewhere!"

Ida leaned on the long-handled broom, crooking an imperious finger. "I wanna see you."

Skinny hopped over the fence, sat on the edge of the sandbox, and dribbled sand through his fingers. "Are ya mad at me, Ida? You look mad."

"Nope. But I'm worried 'bout you. You goin' to be transferred if you don't settle down to makin' your teachers happy."

"I don't care."

"What's that little book you carrying?"

"It's private. My ideas."

"What kinda ideas?"

"Ida, could you lend me a dollar?"

"What for?"

"I lost my lunch money and I'm sure hungry." Skinny looked into Ida's face. "That's really true."

Ida reached into a deep, dress pocket and drew out a frayed brown change purse. "Here's a dollar and some change. You pay me back when you can."

"Thanks, Ida. I'll pay you back next week." He did, and then for weeks Ida didn't see him.

Sometime later, Skinny's private notebook ended up in Mrs. Langley's desk drawer beside a large, shallow box labeled Collateral, in which lay a trick ring, a bracelet, a balloon, and four glassy marbles. In order to stabilize her dwindling pencil supply, Mrs. Langley had instituted with her class a rather simple banking procedure: each time a kid borrowed a pencil (and a day didn't pass without several borrowers), he or she had to put up collateral for it. When the pencil was returned, the kid's possession was given back. Mrs. Langley, shrewd old hand that she was, never allowed herself to be fooled into taking something from a kid that he wouldn't want returned, such as a library book or a badge that said "I Am a Good Citizen." She insisted on precious objects as collateral, such as a house key or a lucky penny. Her pencils flew back to her as regularly as homing pigeons.

Ida actually had no reason for opening and rummaging through this drawer; it was out-of bounds. But perhaps she was looking for another typed-up report on Skinny. Once she had ignored these educational appraisals—except to flick a feather duster over them— but for over a year now, she had divided her work time between cleaning and researching. Ida had no plan, but she found herself irresistibly attracted to the various kinds of accounts teachers draw up regarding their students. These handwritten paragraphs fascinated Ida —and they confused her. The children described in the pages she read did not at all resemble the kids she met and joked with in halls and in the yard, especially Skinny. Ida came to respect the power of words; for Language in the hands of teachers could transform an ordinary kid into a Disturbed Element. Ida had never been a reader, but now she gobbled up anecdotal records the way some people devour soap operas. She was no longer content with just those papers she found on top of desk blotters. She ransacked the bottom drawers of desks and opened files that were plainly marked "Private," including Mrs. Langley's Collateral drawer.

Skinny's notebook told her little. Only one page remained, filled with Skinny's hard-to-read handwriting. It appeared to be a list of words under the heading: Wars.

Sumerians
Assyrians
Medes
Persions
Egypshuns
Cretans
Greeks
Phoneeshuns
Romans
Turks
Mongols

Obviously, Skinny Malinky was a kid with ideas.

During that year at Ripley Street School, Ida followed Skinny's progress through a variety of official documents on various desks: teachers', the vice-principal's (a larger desk, with blotter and nameplate), and the principal's (the largest, with blotter, nameplate, gold pen and pencil). All these numerous reports told Ida that Skinny had run out of time at Ripley Street School. He was to be transferred to another institution—Scratchland. Scratchland was for hopeless kids who would never achieve an "A" spelling paper, a well-written sentence, or an independent project. She would miss Skinny. She hoped Skinny would find her before leaving Ripley Street School.

At the tag end of a Friday afternoon, Skinny popped into his old kindergarten room, where Ida was unsuccessfully wiping a large purplish paint spot off a wall.

"Purple's hard to get out," commented Skinny.

"Remember, Skinny, when you was in this room?"

"That was a long time ago. Give me that sponge for a minute, Ida."

Ida passed Skinny the grayish yellow sponge. Skinny spat neatly in its center. Then he pressed the sponge to the paint spot and rubbed hard. Lo and behold, the color faded!

"My! Who woulda thought it!" Ida laughed, but her eyes remained serious.

"My spit's strong."

Ida mumbled something in her throat. As she continued working, Skinny followed her about.

Several minutes went by. Skinny moved to the blackboard and drew a long chalk line from one end of it to the other. "Know what this is, Ida?"

"Nope."

"It's a time line." Skinny plucked at it with his chalk, making short lines across it. "Know what these little cross lines mean?"

"Nope. You tell me."

"Ee-vents. Things that happened in history. Like wars."

"Wars ain't done anyone no good."

"Ida, do you ever think on how many wars there's been?"

"Nope."

"Well, I figured there musta been about a couple million. Big wars, I mean, not skimpy battles. An' y'know what makes 'em all the same, Ida?"

Ida leaned against a table and drew a breath. "Sure. People wanted somethin'. And took it."

"People. That's right. *People.*" And Skinny put his index finger to his mouth and bit off a piece of skin, then spat it out. "People made all the wars. People, Ida. Not *kids.* I'm going away," he said suddenly.

Ida put her mop down. "I know. To Scratchland."

"How'd you know?"

"Oh, I find out. Guess I won't see you anymore."

Another silence.

"C'mere. I got somethin' for you." Ida held out a palm. Something fiery shone from its center.

"What is it, Ida?"

"It's my old keepsake. I got it when I was your age and kept it ever since."

Skinny took the tiny, glass rabbit between his fingers. It stood on its two hind legs, listening to the wind. It was frosted, and a bright orange glowed from beneath the cloudy surface.

"What happened to its ear?"

"It got chipped because I dropped it. But that's good."

"Why?"

"Because it's been through things. And it's wise. It knows nothin' perfect lasts long."

"I like it." Skinny rubbed it on his cheek. "Are you really giving it to me, Ida?"

"Yep. It's my good luck. I want you to keep it for me."

"Oh Ida, I couldn't take your good luck."

"You gonna need it, Skinny Malinky." Her hand rested for a moment on the boy's copper hair. "It's strong, too. Like your spit." And she smiled. "I got all the luck I can handle."

There came an almost inaudible "Thanks" as the freckled arm drilled down into a pocket, jiggled, and came up with a tiny object that looked like a rigid piece of spiderweb.

"You take *this*, Ida. It's my best thing."

She rolled it around in her hand. "What is it?"

"It's a claw from a blackbird. It always brings me luck."

Ida's eyes blazed up, wrapped themselves around Skinny, then let go.

Skinny raced from the room.

3

Scratchland School

Scratchland was a big school and an old one. The wooden floors had buckled, making hills and valleys across each room. The teachers had long ago closed their eyes to the bumpy floors, the peeling ceilings, the water fountains that refused to work. They were developing new curricula.

The classrooms were filled with furniture. Whenever a school received new furniture, the old desks and chairs went to Scratchland. There was a chair and table for every kid. Nothing brought water to a Scratchland teacher's eye faster than the pride in seeing every kid *seated*. Even though the chairs were pretty well scarred with carvings of one sort or another ("No sense in sending them *new* chairs, the kids will ruin them anyway"), they held up and stretched in rows across each floor, bumps and all, right up to the blackboard.

The main office was another world. Going there was like going to dinner with a rich relative. There were carpets, vases of flowers on the tables, fresh books on the shelves, and not one desk blotter had an ink spot. Of course, a kid had to wait sometimes five or even ten minutes before a clerk would look up from her desk to ask why he was there. That was all right, because there was always an open candy box to inch oneself toward, or papers on a desk to decipher upside down, or telephone conversations to overhear. Occasionally the door to the principal's office was slightly ajar, and Dr. Pucker could be heard talking to someone about Teaching Strategies for Promoting Children's Thinking, or the Responsibility of Teachers to Maintain Friendly Relations with Janitors, or Why All Staff Must Remain on School Grounds During Prescribed School Hours Unless Accompanied by a Doctor's Note.

At Scratchland there were classes for everybody. For poor kids there was a class called Disadvantaged, and there was a class called Exceptional for kids who were exceptionally different. There was a class called Social Adjustment for kids whose IQ's weren't low enough for EMR (Educable Mentally Retarded) nor high enough for Enrichment. (Kids in Enrichment were disappointed to find out that it had nothing to do with getting rich, but with trips to libraries and museums.) Any kid who was noisy, rude, or anchored down by a low IQ got into Adjustment. (One kid from Enrichment found his way to Adjustment after trying to burn down a museum.)

There were plenty of teachers to go around. If reading scores of four kids took a sudden plunge, lo and behold, a special teacher and class sprouted in twenty-four hours, like a mushroom. There was Remedial I and Remedial II, and one class called the Yes Center, where kids said no. Speech class was called Oral Geography, and it was popular with kids who didn't want to read. Music was learning to identify half notes and whole notes and how to copy a clef signature. Art was being shown how to paint a horizon so that the sky (always blue) and the grass (always green) stayed where they belonged. And there were classes the kids called Bus Stops, transition rooms where kids sat waiting for their IQ's to mature.

There was a class to help kids adjust to kindergarten

and a class to help kindergarten teachers adjust to Scratchland kids. There was a Readiness Room for kids and a Readiness Room for teachers. And in Room 17 a class met every Tuesday at nine o'clock, but nobody except the janitor knew what it was, and he wasn't telling.

Skinny spent his first hour at Scratchland on a bench in the main office. He watched his file travel from one desk to another, carefully observing the faces of those who read the voluminous notes that issued from it in an endless stream. One lady, a pink blonde, sniffed continuously. She would read, then stop to gaze at Skinny, pinch one nostril with her finger, then quickly dive back into the folder. Without a word, the blonde passed the file to a tinted brunette. Skinny noticed she licked her lips every four and a half minutes. She touched the pages gingerly with the tip of a long, cherry red fingernail, as if the pages were germy. Every so often her cheeks would flush, and the hand holding the pages would quiver with what looked like little electric shocks. When she had finished reading, she uttered a barely audible moan, pressed the folder to a very flat chest, and rose and vanished into a room that was labeled Señoritas. The blonde and another lady rapidly followed her.

Skinny had never read the contents of his folder. He knew signatures marched like armies through his file. It was near bursting with recommendations on white forms, blue forms, yellow ones, and even light pink cards with slots punched in them. Skinny sat, patiently listening to what sounded like tongue-cluckings, gasps, and whispers behind the Señoritas door, until Pink Blonde emerged, escorted by her two colleagues. They returned to their desks and straightened their blotters. The blonde turned slowly towards Skinny. She coldly curled a finger at him.

Skinny approached her desk, and was about to sit in

the chair beside it when she raised her hand, palm up, and announced, "You are to report to Room 12 immediately and sign in." She handed him a small white paper, enunciating with great emphasis, *"This is your pass."*

"Pass to what?"

Pink Blonde gazed up at the ceiling, then at Tinted Brunette, and began typing furiously.

Skinny placed a none too clean hand on the edge of her blotter. Tinted Brunette, a more formidable lady than Pink Blonde, quickly rose and, pouring a long look into him, said, "It's a class in Orientation." She paused. "It's learning to orient yourself." Skinny shrugged and walked out.

He figured *orient yourself* might mean trying to act Chinese, but *Orientation* meant Mrs. Jerome. She was a large lady with nothing Oriental about her. She bleached her hair white and wore lots of jewelry because, she said, "It makes the children sit up and take notice." Anyone would sit up and take notice, if a necklace made from somebody's rib cage was pushed in front of his face.

The moment Skinny put his foot in the door, Mrs. Jerome was ready for him. "Class, let's welcome our new boy to New Learning Spaces and Places!" She dragged Skinny around the room, jaws working all the time, introducing him to things as if they were people. The kids in Mrs. Jerome's room shrank just listening to her. Mrs. Jerome, who was an ex-typing teacher, had boundless enthusiasm and spouted millions of long, no-end-in-sight sentences, hardly ever using the same word twice.

"She must've swallowed the dictionary," said Skinny to himself as he took the seat she had introduced to him.

Directly behind Skinny sat Curly, a short kid with a head of cropped black curls. Curly liked to suck his thumb, which didn't bother anyone except his teacher.

Whenever she spotted the thumb disappearing, she would pitch a question at him. Loaded with saliva, the questions whistled past Skinny's ear like Roman candles.

"What's the capital of Connecticut, Curly?"

Out came the thumb. "I don't know, but there's a horse in the state of Mane." (Guffaws from the class.)

"Five demerits," boomed Mrs. Jerome.

In went the thumb.

"You know more sass than any kid I ever met," said Skinny to Curly on the playground that morning at recess. "Don't that woman ever run down?"

"Who—Mrs. Jabber? Nope. Never."

Skinny put a fingernail between his teeth and wrenched a bit of it off. "She's gotta be surprised. If she ever stopped talking, I might think how to grind her to a halt. Yeah. The grinding halt," said Skinny, and he produced a new little notebook.

Mrs. Jerome looked up the next day to find all the kids flagrantly barefoot. This experience might have halted any other teacher—but not Mrs. Jerome. She just changed her unit from Highways and Byways of Mazatlán to Sources of Footwear, and had everyone poking into encyclopedias, straining to find items on moccasins, clogs, welts, etc., while her mouth kept churning out bits and pieces about shoe lasts and the McKay stitching machine.

A few days later, Skinny, Curly, and several other kids brought out their "personal pets" and put them on exhibit. That didn't faze Mrs. Jerome either. She switched from Metals and Minerals of the Old World to Common Parasites of the Human Body so fast, the kids didn't have time to blink. Moreover, it demoralized quite a few kids to see under a microscope what made them scratch. Many took baths that night.

For weeks Mrs. Jerome kept Skinny and Curly on their toes, forcing them to stretch their imaginations. It was maddening to Skinny that whatever appeared to him as particularly low-minded actually turned out to be Social Studies. Mrs. Jerome always won. She couldn't be surprised. With a snap of her fingers, she could reshuffle her program in nothing flat. At some point in teacher training, Mrs. Jerome had learned how to be innovative, and though she did perfectly well with lesson plans, she loved the challenge of chucking them and driving the kids to works of reference.

After two months of trying to shock her, Skinny gave up. He came to class without a disruptive idea in his head—and then it happened! A kindergarten kid tied one end of a rope to Mrs. Jerome's door and the other end to the door of the boys' lavatory across the hall. The doors kept yanking open and banging shut. Mrs. Jerome marched over and took hold of her doorknob exactly when Skinny slammed the lavatory door. Mrs. Jerome fell out into the hall. Because Mrs. Jerome had never found herself at right angles to herself before, she actually opened her mouth in a large **O** and emitted . . . nothing!

The kids watched her yank Skinny up by the scruff of his neck. For three minutes, Mrs. Jerome kept opening her mouth, but nothing came out. Beads of saliva formed on her chin. The kids burst into applause.

However, five minutes later Mrs. Jerome had regained control of herself. The rope was laid out across a table and everyone was deep into Nylon and the Miracle of Synthetic Fibers. That is, everyone but Skinny, who had to inhabit a Learning Space in the lavatory for a full hour. Supplying him with brush and pail of water, Mrs. Jerome gave him the job of washing down one wall of scurrilous sayings. When Skinny refused to do this, Mrs. Jerome said, "If you can't use the brush, then you can use your tongue!" And because Skinny knew Mrs. Jerome didn't expect him to, he did exactly that. He licked the entire wall clean.

That night, Skinny and Curly had a long talk. They sat on a bench behind a backstop in a deserted playing field. Curly was holding his wet thumb in the air, gauging the wind. He chanted:

> Margery Daw on the beach
> Went to swim far out of reach.
> She lost her stockings and everything!
> What do you think she came home in?

"What?" asked Skinny, disinterestedly, for his mind was on other things.

"Twilight," replied Curly cheerily.

Skinny gnawed on a piece of skin near the remains of a fingernail. His tongue was black with the pencil it had licked off the bathroom wall.

"How many words, Skinny, do y'reckon you licked off?"

"About four hundred."

"Holy geophysics!"

"But that Mrs. Jabber's gonna get 'em *all back* one of these days. . . ." Skinny spat out the piece of skin contemptuously.

Curly lay back on the bench and surveyed the stars, tracing a finger in the air.

"Curly, you been in other schools. Did you ever have a good teacher?"

"Once. Miss Nagel. Room 11. But she got bumped—dismissed."

"How come?"

"'Cause she didn't use the same readers the other teachers used. And she forgot to take her register with her out on fire drills. And she always had to be reminded to put her chairs on tables after school. Then they found out she let kids read comic books in class. We even made our *own* comic books. Mine was pretty good—*Sir Vanish, the Magician.*"

Skinny held his small, spiral notebook, flipped pages until he came to a blank, drew out a pencil, wrote something.

"Another meeting, Skin?"

"Yeah. This one is important, Curly. It's a plenum."

Curly sat up in admiration. *"A what?"*

"A *plenum*. That's a Mrs. Jabber word for meeting. High-level. You know that girl in our English class, behind my row?"

"You mean Fritzi? The one with the pictures on her toenails who's always writing poems?"

"Yeah. She belongs to a gang called the Mosquitoes. One of the Mosquitoes wrote up the walls in the bathroom. Fritzi said she was sorry about what Mrs. Jabber made me do, but she was glad *I* got the words and the soap and bucket didn't."

Curly whooped, and Skinny joined in.

"There's another gang, too, Curly. Called Peanut Butter and Jam. There are enough of us for a war, Curly. It's time kids took over the schools."

"My dad was in a war. He was drafted."

"Well, we don't need to draft kids. They'll volunteer." Skinny wrote for a minute, with Curly looking over his shoulder. *Strategies. Skirmishes. Invasion.*

"You need lots of friends for an invasion, Skinny. An *army* of friends."

"That's right." After a pause, Skinny added: "We're gonna declare war. You and me."

Curly exhaled noisily, then extended his hand. Skinny took it in his own.

And that was the beginning.

4

The Teachers Confer

The following weeks at Scratchland School were hard on teachers. Every day something outrageous happened. First, someone started fooling with the flags; not the national or state flags, but more important, the school flags. These flags didn't have any special insignia or coat of arms on them. Plain colored squares of cheesecloth—red, yellow, blue, and green—they were important in keeping track of the day's weather and Dr. Pucker's disposition.

Dr. Pucker, Scratchland's principal, believed in clockwork, a trim sail, round holes for round pegs, and flags. When the yellow flag was out it meant Eat In, Play Out (it was raining, but not bad enough that the teachers had to stay in with the kids). A red flag meant Eat In, Play In (too wet out for teachers). A green flag meant Eat Out, Play Out (the sun was shining). Blue meant No Eating, No Playing (School Board visiting).

One Monday, the red flag was posted on the fence. That puzzled the teachers, because the sun was out. Just to make sure, they kept their classes in for lunch. Then, as everyone sat down to eat, the green flag was posted and all classes had to go out. Then the blue flag was displayed, and teachers had to scramble to get their classes in again and clean up their rooms because the School Board had a way of looking under tables for wads of gum. So, of course, the blue flag not only meant No Eating, No Playing, but tugging gum from dark and sticky corners. Curly called it "milking the cow," and the Mosquitoes drove teachers wild with bovine mooing.

Then a note came from the office saying, "Ignore previous flags. Resume schedule." There was a good deal of teacher room-hopping to determine where they were in the schedule. Was it time for lunch, physical education, or academic skills? Teachers whispered and gesticulated in the halls, trying to synchronize themselves, so at least they'd all make the same mistake.

The next day, Dr. Pucker had every flag under lock and key, but it started again, this time with a new flag. It was bluish green or greenish blue, and the teachers couldn't agree on its meaning. Some rooms Ate Out, Played Out; some opted for No Eating, No Playing. One class, to be on the safe side, took a field trip. The new flag, you can be sure, made everyone uneasy—except for the art teacher, Mr. Heather, who said he was sure the flag was turquoise and "perfectly lovely."

The third day nothing unusual happened.

"Let 'em slide back to normal," said Skinny. "We'll hit 'em when they least expect it."

The following morning was punctuated by the bell ringing three short rings every ten seconds.

"Take cover! Take cover!" yelled the teachers.

Everyone crouched under chairs and tables, heads between knees. Suddenly, the bell rang long and steadily.

"Fire!" shouted the teachers, dragging the kids up and marshaling them out to the yard. When they were outside, the bell broke its rhythm and abruptly rang the signal for Tornado, and the kids and teachers ran pell-mell for the basement. Then the bell stopped. As everyone filed back into classrooms, the Emergency Drop bell sounded, loud and clear. Everyone dropped hard in a prone position, arms covering face. One teacher dropped with such zeal that his chest was painfully punctured by his tie tack.

All in all it was a trying week. Visibly shaken, Mrs. Jerome visited her old aunt. Mrs. Solemnsides, a retired elocution teacher, lived in a trailer camp with her Pekinese lapdog, Snitch.

"It's a declaration of war, Auntie, I just know it," said Mrs. Jerome. "You know, I was at Faultfinder Junior High when it broke out there. The kids rang the civil defense siren, got all the teachers into the fallout shelters, locked them in, and then proceeded to . . . ssssssssss." Her voice dropped to a whisper.

"What's that, dear?" Old Mrs. Solemnsides shifted Snitch to her other knee and bent closer to Mrs. Jerome. "You don't say!" she cried. "That's perfectly awful!"

"I can read the signs," said Mrs. Jerome. "It's coming."

"What's coming, dear?" asked Mrs. Solemnsides.

"Never mind," said Mrs. Jerome. "Just come to my room tomorrow after class. We teachers are getting together to see if we can do something about it."

"Why of course, dear," replied Mrs. Solemnsides, who was very pleased at the invitation. The thought of seeing desks and chairs and blackboards again put roses in her cheeks.

The following afternoon, several teachers met in Mrs. Jerome's room. Mr. Skourinotz, the civics teacher, arrived first. He was a slight, quiet man who had been a farmer and was very knowledgeable on the subject of poultry, especially fowl diseases like turkey blackhead and cecal coccidiosis. His classes learned a vast amount about breeding swine and desexing chickens along with democratic processes.

Next to show up was Mr. Bullotad, the gym teacher. He was a muscular man who once had been a champion gymnast. Now his most prominent muscle was his stomach, which hung over his gym shorts and was useful for butting kids into the showers. In the evening Mr. Bullotad taught Police Practices: Beginning and Intermediate, and Vice Control: Lower Division at the local junior college.

Also present were Miss Jenny Dunphy and her twin sister, Miss Bambi Dunphy. They were known as the Dumpy sisters, and Miss Bambi had become Miss Bumpy. The Dunphys taught Morals and Manners, and were in hot water with the school administration because they came to class with all kinds of newfangled ideas from child psychology books which hadn't been put on the Approved Books list.

Mr. Snockadocka, the new English teacher, and Mrs. Primrose, the vice-principal, came last.

Mr. Snockadocka was a fanatic on The New Grammar. He was one of three men in the entire world who could understand the school textbooks on linguistics. He had a way of protruding his lower lip and quivering it to show disapproval. This was his first semester at Scratchland, and the teachers didn't know much about him except that he displayed his lower lip frequently, he carried his own custom-made chalk with steel centers wherever he went, and Henry Wadsworth Longfellow was his favorite poet.

Mrs. Primrose had been vice-principal for eighteen years. She had taken the principal's exam seventeen times and failed each time. Perhaps, because she was the only person who knew where the ditto paper was stored and did not want to relinquish this important responsibility, she purposely kept flunking the exam.

Old Mrs. Solemnsides had been in Mrs. Jerome's room since noon. She sat balancing on her lap a large embroidery basket, from which her dog Snitch poked his unfriendly head. She was a great fan of Mrs. Jerome's and wanted to become her teacher's aide. Mornings she worked as a receptionist at the Four-Footed Heaven Pet Cemetery, and afternoons she spent with the Antivivisection Glee Club.

After everyone had greeted the beaming Mrs. Solemnsides and poured coffee, Mr. Skourinotz started the discussion. "I think a good course in animal husbandry might help. It would be jim-dandy for many of our children. I would be willing to take a limited number for a class in The Control of Bacterial Wilt and Mexican Firebrats."

"It won't work," boomed out Mr. Bullotad. "Just look what happened in your class last year. Strawberry diseases, wasn't it? And by God, the whole school got that miserable skin rash!"

"True," responded Mrs. Jerome. "Things have gone too far for that!"

"You know how I feel," cut in Mr. Bullotad. "There's nothing like a good old-fashioned physical-fitness program to straighten out troublemakers. Run them ragged, fill the day with standing broad jumps, shot puts, push-ups, and the fifty-yard dash, plus some other real hard stunts. That'll do it."

Old Mrs. Solemnsides nodded vigorously. She had been a great sportswoman when young, and still excelled in games of acey-deucey, crambo, and snipsnapsnorum.

"Excellent," said Mrs. Primrose, "but we mustn't lose sight of their minds. I cannot believe there exists a child who isn't worth saving."

After a lengthy silence, she continued. "At Quasimodo State Teachers College, where I trained, we made several pilot studies on minimizing conflicts between child and teacher. We found that phenobarbital brought the children down to a suitable level for learning and helped the teachers, also, in relating to them."

"My opinion . . ." said Mr. Snockadocka, and everyone turned to him, "is that the new Princeton T.T.T.D. will work wonders here."

"What's Princeton T.T.T.D.?" asked Mrs. Primrose.

"Well . . ." and Mr. Snockadocka laughed shamefacedly. "When I was a graduate student, we made up

that phrase among ourselves. Testing Them To Death."
Everyone tittered, and he blushed. "Seriously, though,
it's been tried at many schools with marvelous results.
There's a new thematic apperception test that runs for
eighteen hours and is administered by qualified counse-
lors in armored tanks."

Suddenly, Mr. Skourinotz, who was only four feet,
nine inches tall, stood on a chair and shouted, "The
trouble is there's NO RESPECT!"

Then Miss Jenny Dunphy spoke up. "We must avoid
abbreviated or slang expressions which may offend
members of ethnic groups, such as *chink, jap, flip, frog,
greaser, wop, guinea, heeb,* and *pickaninny.*"

"Yes," emphatically agreed her twin sister, Miss
Bambi Dunphy. "And we must shun ethnic adjectives
even when giving praise, such as 'He is a nice colored
man.'"

Mrs. Jerome looked impatient. Her mouth sizzled
like a fuse. The clock read 3:30, a bell rang, and the
teachers raced out the door, looking neither to the right
nor to the left. All the teachers entered their cars and
zoomed out of the parking lot, leaving a great cloud of
exhaust fumes floating over the school yard.

5

The Storm Begins

Several important things about Mr. Snockadocka were circulated via the school grapevine. Number one: he collected first editions of Longfellow's work. A large portrait of the poet hung above his desk. Number two: he believed in charts. He was full professor of graphs at Saint Solipsis for the Foreign-Born, and had authored a series of textbooks on English for children all the way from nursery school to twelfth grade. His linguistic tables were famous. Wherever English teachers gathered, they talked like the tables in Mr. Snockadocka's books, saying things like *"Q front plus noun phrase plus tense plus be plus ing plus bother plus George."* (That means "Do you know what is bothering George?") Another teacher would reply, *"Indefinite adverbial of place plus auxiliary plus modal plus verbal plus determiner plus intensifier plus particle plus copula."* (That means "No.")

Principals hadn't the vaguest notion of what Mr. Snockadocka's books meant, but they were visibly affected by the uniformity and neat precision of his sentence diagrams. On leave from St. Solipsis, Mr. Snockadocka had been deluged by offers to work in various schools. He had eventually chosen Scratchland "Because," he said, "it holds a remarkable *mix* and is a challenge to any educator."

To tell the truth, Mr. Snockadocka had chosen Scratchland because Dr. Pucker promised him an unlimited supply of felt pens and gave Mr. Snockadocka his own key to the men's room.

Mr. Snockadocka was a good-looking young man except for his protruding lower lip and a sloping, dead-white forehead upon which two blue veins meandered. He dressed fastidiously, in the latest fashion. Along with a stunning collection of sport jackets, Mr. Snockadocka brought with him to Scratchland his tables and charts of Trees of Derivation. These were his most prized possessions. Resource teachers looked upon them as works of art and made slides of them. One language arts resource teacher, a Miss Whippany, referred to those charts on which Mr. Snockadocka had used a blue felt pen as belonging to Mr. Snockadocka's Blue Period. Of course, Mr. Snockadocka was very flattered. Every few months Mr. Snockadocka changed the color of his felt pen, and Miss Whippany never failed to comment on his new Period.

Mr. Snockadocka loved sentences. He believed in sentences. The kids at Scratchland used amazingly original sentences. Mr. Snockadocka itched to explicate those sentences, to show each kid how he or she was using negatives, affirmatives, past and present tenses, progressive forms, and past participles. He believed that any kid who could learn to produce a proper sentence and break it down could become a responsible adult. Being new to kids in a classroom, Mr. Snockadocka displayed a world of patience. No sentence stopped him. Mr. Snockadocka was inventive enough to transform into formulas such verses as:

> Papa Moses caught a skunk,
> Mama Moses cooked a chunk,

Baby Moses ate a hunk,
Holy Moses, how he stunk!

The veins in his forehead throbbed busily as he put arrows and plus signs in his charts.

Skinny overheard the following conversation outside Mr. Snockadocka's door late one afternoon.

"I'd like to acquaint you with how I like my room prepared for the next day. You're new here, am I correct?"

"That right. I take Mr. Slade's rooms."

It was a familiar voice. Skinny's lips parted, then relaxed into a small smile.

"It's my chalk trays," said Mr. Snockadocka.

"Hm-m."

"I like them im*ma*culate."

"Mm-mmm . . ."

"I don't like teensy-weensies scattered about."

"What you mean?"

"I mean, nothing disturbs me more than pygmies amongst the chalk family. The kids put them in their pockets or their mouths or stomp on them and scatter them."

"You mean loose ends a' chalk?"

"That's right."

"You want me to throw all these little pieces away?"

"That's what I've been talking about. Yes."

"Somebody sure could do a lot of writin' with these pieces."

"And *furthermore,* I've noticed that Mr. Slade has been remiss on locking up my Trees—my charts here."

"Lock up? Where to?"

"They should be taken to the supply room by the main office."

"You mean you want me to carry all these card-boards over to the main office each night?"

"These 'cardboards' are most precious."

43

"I'm just curious but I'd like to know, how come they can't be happy locked up in this room?"

"Scratchland is different from other schools you've worked in, I'm sure. Take my word for it."

Skinny slid around a corner as Mr. Snockadocka strode out of his door. Then he tiptoed back and looked inside. He whispered, "Ida!"

A jubilant look spread over Ida's face. "I mighta known my Skinny Malinky bump inta me!"

"What are you doing here?"

"Same as ever as old Ida does. I a sub, now."

"A sub?"

"Yep. I take the place of sick janitors. They gonna fire me last year but made me a sub."

Skinny looked angry. "Why were they gonna fire you? You work so hard!"

"Budget cut, Skinny. But I was offered a sub job, so I take it." Ida studied the freckled face before her. "I hear a' you, Skinny, from time to time. You gettin' famous. You and a couple other kids givin' teachers rough times."

Skinny wandered over to the chart rack and gazed at Mr. Snockadocka's Trees of Derivation.

"You still filled up with war ideas?" Ida asked.

Skinny sat on a table, drew up his knees, and hugged them. "It's growing inside of me, Ida. I can't stop it."

"Well. Things gotta run their course, but war is a terrible trouble. It gonna hurt you."

"I know it," Skinny said quietly. And after a minute, he drew out the tiny, glass rabbit from a pocket and held it up. They stared solemnly at one another. Skinny slid off the table, waved, and was gone.

The next day in Skinny's English class, Mr. Snockadocka rose from his desk under Longfellow's portrait. With a tragic face, he waved a paper in the air. "Last week's assignment, as you all know, was to compose three short poems in meter and rhyme. I should like to share Mr. Malinky's contribution with you now."

The kids stirred. Skinny, slumped in his seat, sat up.

"The first poem, I believe, is entitled 'Thirsty.'"

> thermos saint bernard (with no capitals)
> tongue saint bernard
> snake saint bernard
> car saint bernard
> and numbers to dial a saint bernard
> when
> you
> don't
> have
> drinking fountens (spelled with an *e*)
> and you got mouth emergency.

Mr. Snockadocka paused. The class tittered. Skinny scowled.

> shadows are like bugs in the sky.
> clouds are full of flees. (no *a* in fleas)
> shake out the pillows someone say
> but don't loose feathers
> or you'll get beat up
> for sky losing.

Skinny's face and freckles were blood-red. The tittering stopped.

"And the last one goes like this:

> Gages (another misspelling), pages,
>   books and tractors.
> Many parts. I think there is
> a driver for a book.
>   guess where he goes?
>   into your head
>   over bumpy roads.

A book can dig. Drive, driver, drive.
seed drop from book."

Mr. Snockadocka looked up. "Not only are these contributions sadly lacking in meter and rhyme, but they are distinguished by a lamentable lack of correct spelling, punctuation, and syntax. Beginning words in a sentence are willy-nilly capitalized, sentences move in and out of the page like cars out of control, and nowhere is there a coherent thought or poetic idea that makes sense." The veins in Mr. Snockadocka's forehead pulsed as he leaned forward. "I believe, Mr. Malinky, you have written a little masterpiece of error. I have never seen an assignment so brutally bludgeoned to death."

Silence. Everyone was looking back at Skinny, in the last row.

Mr. Snockadocka, his lips set in a twisted smile, met Skinny's angry expression head-on. "Waste Not, Want Not is one of my mottos," he said. "These three poems remain so incredible as bad examples that I shall incorporate them into my newest chart and have them prominently displayed at my next seminar for teachers."

Skinny stood up. Slowly, he placed his finger in his mouth, took out a piece of gum, and flicked it into the air. The gum landed exactly on the left eye of Henry Wadsworth Longfellow and hung there.

A gasp came from the class.

Mr. Snockadocka turned crimson, and his lower lip seemed to go out of control.

"This here's an oration of war," said Skinny. He turned and walked out.

Several other kids rose, glared defiantly at Mr. Snockadocka, and followed Skinny out of the room.

6

Skinny's Revenge

Among those who walked out of Mr. Snockadocka's class were Curly and Fritzi, a tall girl who wore a soiled navy pea jacket, a Hawaiian grass skirt, red leotards, and tap-dancing shoes. They followed Skinny to an open field near the school.

"I talked to my friend Alma at Rockinghorse School," said Fritzi, polishing first one shoe, then the other against its opposite ankle. "All the kids are practicing."

"Practicing what?" asked Skinny.

Fritzi winked. "Practicing *maneuvers*. Joey Mandelbaum at Mimeo has a whole slew of recruits."

Skinny bit his lip. "Mimeo—is that a school?"

"Uh-huh. Not far from here. It's really Pangloss Polytechnic, but we call it Mimeo. The kids run that school. The teachers are so busy at the copy machines they don't know what's going on."

Curly drew a slice of gum from a pocket, tore it into three equal parts, and handed out two.

"Fritzi," asked Skinny, "do you know any of the kids in Peanut Butter and Jam?"

"All of 'em. They're really gross," she said admiringly.

47

"How gross?" asked Curly.

Fritzi opened her pea jacket to hitch up her skirt. "Well, Judy Johnston put a goldfish in the office water cooler and Mr. Screwy Nuts swallowed it. Alec Wampkins slid a potato bug in the sweatband of Mr. Bullet Head's hat. And Brian Lodesmith put thirty-six night crawlers in Mrs. Pig Nose's handbag." Fritzi gave out with a tiny, apologetic sigh. "They're all insect buffs, interested in the reactions of urban dwellers to entomological phenomena."

Skinny and Curly hee-heeed.

Curly popped his thumb out of his mouth. Gum sat on the thumb like a wart. "That was some trick, Skinny, in Mr. Snockadocka's room. Your aim was terrific."

Skinny ignored the compliment. "Can you figger out a way, Curly, to get into the Scratchland supply room without being seen?"

"I can make a wax impression and produce a key, if that would be satisfactory. How about a pact, Skinny? I could draw up a real fancy concordat."

"What's that?"

"It's what kings and popes signed when they agreed to be allies and fight together against the infidel."

Curly produced a roll of butcher paper, which he laid out with a flourish. Skinny's and Fritzi's mouths hung open in admiration. The paper was a dazzling display of ornate printing and vine-leaf design.

"It's great, Curly! You're an artist!" said Fritzi.

"Yeah. It looks like a real treaty!"

The concordat was written in a thick black ink and was illuminated with luminous gold and silver paint. It read:

BE IT RESOLVED THAT the War between the Pitiful Teachers and the Splendid Kids be waged in the Name

48

of Justice, Truth, Freedom, and Full Replenishment of Those Inalienable Rights given to All Kids by Bountiful Nature. The Aforementioned War to be led and conducted by These Leaders Illustrious:

[There followed a row of blank lines.]

These Leaders shall be empowered to call to Arms All Those Kids ready, willing, and able to give Their Service and Talents and shall provide Divers Weapons and Armaments and Tactics to coordinate Offensive and Defensive Strategies, to engage in Raids, Forays, Sieges, and Various and General Beleaguerments against said Teachers, anywhere and everywhere until said Enemies of Kids be irremediably Vanquished, Mastered, Subdued, Crushed, Humbled, Brought to Their Knees, and Trampled Underfoot. And a Just and Lasting Peace be Initiated Forever for All Kids everywhere.

Below these lines flowered a large, golden seal with two blue ribbons attached. The seal, slightly used, had these words on it: MISS RUTH'S ARM AND HAMMER NURSERY SCHOOL.

Curly held out a pin. Skinny pricked his finger, and as the drop of blood fell on the paper, he scratched his name on the first blank line. Curly, then Fritzi, followed suit.

Curly stole the key to the school supply room, made a copy of it, and returned the original—all in the space of two hours, so no one suspected any mischief. In the room lay a year of supplies for the Scratchland staff. But it was Mr. Snockadocka's grammer charts which Skinny wanted.

Mr. Snockadocka's remarkable charts represented years of philosophical thought—years of doing without shaving lotion to pay for courses, books, chart paper, and pencils, pens, and rulers. These charts were Mr. Snockadocka's pyramids, memorials to his talent and industry. They were really all he lived for. He dated only those women who, in his words, could "accept the possibility of a universal grammar and generate sentences of deep structure."

Skinny and Curly were absent the day Mr. Snockadocka learned about the theft of his charts. The Mosquitoes, who made up a majority of this particular class, were there in full force. At the blackboard, Mr. Snockadocka was laboriously diagramming sentences which the Mosquitoes contributed. Mr. Snockadocka's most brilliant diagramming resulted when Fritzi, told to shut her mouth, snapped back with "Shut your own, it's closer."

Mr. Snockadocka stepped back to survey his work, and discovered that he had invented a new symbol. A delightful shiver went up his spine. Peering at the blackboard, Mr. Snockadocka confirmed that instead of drawing his customary arrow, thusly ⟶ , he had unwittingly drawn ⟶ . He had been searching for a symbol to express a new step in grammatical process which had been forming in his head for three months. He could hardly contain his happiness. Running his fingers through his rich head of hair and pushing out his lower lip in an expression of "Aha! *Now* look at what I've done!" he buzzed for Dr. Pucker.

As Mr. Snockadocka was discovering his ⟶ , Dr. Pucker was busily labeling boxes for brass fasteners, scratch pads, art gum erasers, thumbtacks, and rubber bands. Although all these supplies came in their own boxes, it disturbed Dr. Pucker to see so many different sizes and shapes cluttering the shelves. He repacked all these items into custom-made containers of uniform size. The contents of each was printed in a fine, legible hand on labels which were stuck carefully on two sides of each container. Dr. Pucker had saved the jumbo paper clips for last, and was about to start on them when he heard the insistent buzz from Mr. Snockadocka's room. He ignored it, but it sounded again. Two sharp lines like red scars appeared between his eyebrows.

As Dr. Pucker left his office, his secretary handed him a note from the Security Force. It told of the theft of Mr. Snockadocka's charts. Dr. Pucker returned to his office, picked up his civil defense helmet, and raced to Mr. Snockadocka's room.

Fritzi stood and saluted smartly as he entered. The principal ignored her. Mr. Snockadocka, pointing with pride to his new symbol, read the awful expression in Dr. Pucker's face and let his arm fall slowly down to his side.

"What is it, sir?" he asked in a low voice.

After casting a long, accusing look at the silent class, Dr. Pucker announced, "There has been a theft."

The Mosquitoes looked coolly at Dr. Pucker.

Dr. Pucker drew himself up as tall as he could ("making eye contact," as he liked to put it), and intoned, "Continued willful disobedience, open, persistent defiance of authority, habitual profanity and vulgarity, willfully cutting, defacing, or otherwise injuring in any way any property, real or personal, by theft or otherwise, belonging to a school district; also, joining or becoming a member of any secret fraternity, sorority, or club wholly or partly formed from the membership of pupils attending the public schools, for the purpose of seriously disturbing the discipline of administrative regulations and Board rulings, shall be punishable by demotion, suspension, expulsion, or, if necessary, referral to proper official penal institutions, for the sole purpose of proper supervision and correctional administration of deviant behavior without possible future reinstatement privileges from the Student Reclamation Pilot Study and Christian Salvage Program."

If Mr. Snockadocka had had any anxiety concerning what had been stolen from the supply room, it was wiped away during Dr. Pucker's speech. A fellow man—neither a linguist nor an English major, but a teacher, an *administrating* teacher—had uttered in his presence the *longest sentence ever spoken*. It was devastating, the mightiest challenge Mr. Snockadocka had ever faced. But before he could grab his chalk and begin his step-by-step analysis of Dr. Pucker's incredible sentence, the Mosquitoes slammed their books down on their desks and banged them in rhythm. Then an arm materialized through an open window. Attached to the arm was a hand. In the hand was a brown paper bag. And in the bag were dozens of black beetles, commonly known as stinkbugs. The inside of the bag was torn open and the beetles flew into the room.

The War had begun.

7

Two Crucial Meetings

Dr. Pucker and Mr. Snockadocka went into hiding in the supply room.

"They can't be deported as aliens, and they're too young to be shot into space," muttered Mr. Snockadocka. "I wonder if we ought to contact the parents."

"Parents? It would be a waste of time," replied Dr. Pucker. "You'll never pry them loose from their TV screens." He shook his head. "The Board of Education is putting tremendous pressure on me. They're worried about the effect that Skinny Malinky is having on the neighboring schools. Mr. Foreclosure, the chairman, is—"

"Mr. Foreclosure! The mysterious financier?"

"Yes. He sits on the Scratchland Board, or his trusted agent Sterling Guts does. I've never met him, but he called me this morning to set up a meeting. We are going to get some help."

"From whom, sir?"

"Colonel Kratz. Ever hear of him?"

"Kratz? Of course! He put down a Kids' war a few years ago at Mount Rushmore. The Kids had stolen Lincoln's nose and Roosevelt's chin. Or was it the other way round?" asked Mr. Snockadocka.

"That sounds minor compared to the Kids' war Kratz handled at the Twisted Umlaut School for Unbalanced Girls at Mount Chagrin, Nebraska."

Both the English teacher and the principal felt much more optimistic. Dr. Pucker called a teachers' conference two nights later. He persuaded the teachers to cancel their bridge games, their book club discussion groups, and all social activities. Dr. Pucker remembered that teachers were always ready to widen their academic horizons, so he offered 1 (one) college credit for attending the meeting.

All the teachers showed up. Along with Mr. Snockadocka, there were Mr. Skourinotz, Mr. Bullotad, old Mrs. Solemnsides and her lapdog, Snitch, Miss Jenny Dunphy and her twin sister, Miss Bambi Dunphy, Mrs. Primrose, and Mrs. Jerome. And there was a stranger —Colonel Kratz.

Colonel Kratz wore thick-lensed glasses and a melancholy mien. In three short years he had risen from playground aide to superintendent of schools for the Unified School District of Rollover, Connecticut, and he was looked upon with great awe by everyone.

Colonel Kratz talked for a long time. He punctuated his speech with such memorable phrases as "A privilege, not a right," "All pupils shall be required to," "The following measures shall be taken," "No person under the age of," "Your duty as a teacher," "Corporal punishment may be administered in cases when," and "Meeting the child's emotional needs." Colonel Kratz's speech was so moving (and salivary) that there wasn't a dry eye in the audience when he finished.

At the same time, Skinny, Curly, and Fritzi met in a tree outside Scratchland, to discuss the chart theft. A stranger had been sitting in the tree when Curly arrived, and he invited her to stay because she refused to leave.

Big Alice Eyesore had always been a problem. At four weeks of age, she had fifteen of her permanent teeth, all canines, and she did terrible damage to her crib toys. Her father, Dr. Eyesore, was a psychiatrist, and Mrs. Eyesore was a psychiatric social worker. They were afraid of her, but they tried all kinds of techniques to help Alice become a pleasant and rational member of human childhood.

Before she was one year old, Big Alice had been run through all the major tests: the Piotr Ilyich Sex Role Blur, the Gunderson Fishing Quest Cards, and the Cardona-Hine Haiku Search. Big Alice was initiated into planned ignoring, permissive interdiction, and pressurized-cabin–theory therapy. Nothing worked. Big Alice was completely unmanageable. Her parents, driven to desperation, drove out to the Lake Cachuma Wildlife Preserve and left her there with a month's supply of diapers, half a dozen jumbo safety pins, and two cases of formula.

A hyena adopted her. This hyena had just lost a cub, and her maternal instincts were in high gear. Rudy, her nephew, became Big Alice's constant playmate. Big Alice thrived. As years passed, she grew a bit of a tail, and that pleased her.

Just as Big Alice was about to become a real hyena, her parents came looking for her. It wasn't because Dr. and Mrs. Eyesore were sorry about leaving their only offspring in the woods and were trying to make amends, for they had never for one moment felt any qualms. It was simply a matter of research. What better subject for research papers could there be than Big Alice? Dr. Eyesore planned to call his paper "Programming for Ego Support: The Viability of Early Child Desertion." Mrs. Eyesore planned to entitle hers "Jungle Foster Homes: Hide-and-Seek Therapy, A New Procedure."

Dr. Eyesore had an Eagle Scout badge in knots, so it wasn't difficult for him to trap Big Alice. Trap her he did, with two half hitches and a fisherman's eye. What a grim moment that was! For the first few days, the two Eyesores almost gave up writing their papers and instead considered selling Big Alice to a promoter for a flashy commercial enterprise. Big Alice's parents could have enriched themselves and become instantly famous, but they decided to bring Big Alice home to live quietly with them. They even sent her to school.

The schools that Big Alice attended were never the same after she'd spent time in them. A high percentage of Big Alice's teachers left teaching to go into other fields. In fact, just a hint that Big Alice was expected in a school was enough to cut a sudden, wide swath in the teaching personnel. Such was the case when Alice enrolled at Scratchland.

One teacher for whom Big Alice held no threat was Mrs. Jerome. This was not because Mrs. Jerome was a particularly brave woman or because Big Alice represented an unusual Social Studies unit. Mrs. Jerome was convinced that she could change Big Alice into a real, human girl. "If I can teach Big Alice to type thirty words a minute and take shorthand," she mused, "think of what an accomplishment that would be!" Mrs. Jerome dreamed of the day when she and Big Alice would walk hand in hand into Dr. Pucker's office. Big Alice would sit and take dictation from the principal. Dr. Pucker would rise and shake Mrs. Jerome by the hand, congratulating her. . . .

Curly was tremendously impressed by Big Alice's appearance. When Skinny and Fritzi arrived, they were enchanted. Alice was better than the horror movies on TV.

"I *adore* the hair on the back of your neck, Big Alice," Fritzi said. "May I . . . touch it?"

"Sure," replied Big Alice, in a voice that reminded Skinny of a motor being revved up.

Fritzi stroked Big Alice's neck gingerly, then shivered. "Oh! *Diabolical!*"

"What's that?" asked Big Alice, scratching her armpits.

"It means super-great," exclaimed Fritzi, her face flushed with admiration.

"Are you going to be at Scratchland?" asked Skinny.

"Yeah. When my parents don't keep me busy."

"Doing what?" asked Curly.

"I got a paper route. And I'm scraping paint off my parents' walls." Big Alice laughed a gruesome-sounding laugh. "I do it with my teeth." She opened her mouth.

Fritzi drew closer and squealed. Big Alice's teeth were green and gray, specked with yellow.

"I also help with her ironing. I drool on the clothes. Wanna see me snarl?"

The kids nodded.

Big Alice snarled. The snarls were noisy and very salivaladen.

"I hate teachers," growled Big Alice. "They're always making me stand up on two feet and wipe my chin." She gazed at Skinny and twitched her nose. "I heard about your war. I'd like to help."

"Do you have any ideas, Big Alice?" asked Curly.

"Well, I learned about traps at the Lake Cachuma Wildlife Preserve, where I live in the summertime. We could trap the teachers."

"I like that idea," exclaimed Fritzi. "You mean like a bear trap?"

"Naw. A hole. We dig a hole and cover it, then lay a trail of papers leading to it."

"What kind of papers?" Skinny asked.

"Lists of misspelled words, like *recieve* and *infleckshun* and *hairloom* and *terpentime*."

"How about *pisgetti?*" said Curly.

"And *relinkwish,*" asked Skinny.

"Okay," said Big Alice.

"Then what?" asked Skinny.

"Then we bait the pit, like with the food they serve at school."

"S.O.S.?" suggested Skinny. Fritzi and Curly laughed.

"What's that?"

"Same Old Slush. The other day," said Skinny, thinking hard, "we had hamburger gravy, biscuits, raisin pudding, and milk."

"Crude petroleum, dead babies, scab-and-matter custard, and cow juice," said Curly rapidly.

"Do the teachers eat the same as you?" asked Big Alice.

"Yep," replied Skinny, "except they get bigger portions."

"What did you have last week?"

Curly piped up: "Irish spew."

Skinny shook his head. "It was grilled cheese sandwich on Monday."

"Frizzled hamster between doorsteps," added Curly.

"Then on Tuesday we had spaghetti with butter sauce."

"Filleted string in cement," said Curly.

"What was it on Wednesday?" Skinny asked, turning to Curly.

"Meat pie, green peas, and bread and jelly."

"Dog's dinner, cannonballs, and flies' cemetery."

"On Thursday, I remember, we had macaroni."

"Drainpipes," said Curly.

"And on Friday . . ." Skinny scrunched up his face. "I forget."

"Baked potato," declared Curly. "Rock of Gibraltar."

"Okay, I got the answer," said Big Alice, who had stopped listening.

"Which is?" asked Curly, dodging a blow from Skinny.

"Shark-infested rice pudding."

Everyone shuddered with anticipation.

"I have a shark in my aquarium at home. Her name is Lulu. And she likes rice pudding."

Late that night, Big Alice and Skinny dragged a plastic wading pool with Lulu inside over a deep hole which Fritzi and the Mosquitoes had dug in front of the flagpole. Big Alice and Skinny tied a rope around Lulu and gently lowered her into a large bathtub full of rice pudding at the bottom of the hole. Curly had filled the tub with tomorrow's pudding from the cafeteria.

"Wow! Look at her teeth!" cried Skinny.

"She's smiling. She smiles a lot," said Big Alice, leaning over the pit and waving to Lulu. "My parents gave her to me for my birthday. She'll do anything I tell her."

"What'll she do when the teachers fall in?" asked Curly.

"Heh-heh! Whaddya think!" laughed Big Alice.

Skinny swallowed. And Fritzi wet her lips.

"Where's the papers?" asked Big Alice.

Fritzi produced a satchel and opened it. "I got papers from nearly all the kids. They're all 'F' and 'D' papers."

"Good!" muttered Big Alice, glancing at a paper. "This word has been crossed out and written over four times."

Fritzi leaned over Big Alice's shoulder. "And it's still wrong."

The kids covered the pit and laid a trail with the papers into the Scratchland parking lot. That night they slept in the elm tree nearby.

Mr. Heather, the art teacher, was the first to find the papers the next morning. He was a thin, pimply young man who designed ingenious place mats for Scratchland staff parties. As social chairperson, he sent all the get-well cards and condolence bouquets. Kids took various Appreciation classes with Mr. Heather, but Mr. Heather himself was not much appreciated by the kids.

Mr. Heather picked up one paper, then another. Soon he stood at the very edge of the hole. The kids, in their hiding place, held their breath.

All at once, a breeze came up, and some of the papers that lay over the pit blew off.

"Why, it's a *hole*," cried Mr. Heather, craning his thin neck over it. "And there's something down there!"

59

The kids groaned.

"Why, golly me!" exclaimed Mr. Heather, going down on his knees and squinting. "It looks like old-fashioned shark-infested rice pudding! Like Mom used to make!" And, to the kids' surprise, he jumped in!

The kids rushed over to the pit and gazed down.

"He's eating it," said Big Alice.

"He *likes* it!" exclaimed Skinny disgustedly.

"Yeah," said Curly. "Guess I'm not surprised. I had Mr. Heather for three classes so far, and we got into driftwood, mushroom hunting, quilt-making, sand painting, growing redwoods into bonsai—"

"What's that mean?"

"It means shrinking big things. In his class last year we made gravestone rubbings."

"Weird," said Alice.

Suddenly the shark lifted her great snout.

Mr. Heather whacked it. "Sassy shark!"

The poor, humiliated fish sank to the bottom of the tub and sulked. This was bad enough, but it got worse when Mr. Heather, after eating his fill, began lecturing the large, finny creature on the Aesthetic Experience. The shark, who had never been exposed to an Art Appreciation teacher before, was driven to leap from the pit.

"Poor Lulu," said Big Alice, patting the shark under a fin. "C'mon, help me get her back in the pool."

But before the kids could deposit the shark back in the pool, Fritzi saw someone approaching. The kids hastily hid behind some juniper trees nearby.

It was Mrs. Primrose, jogging through the park to Scratchland. She saw the stranded shark. Being nearsighted, she mistook Lulu for a visiting consultant. Consultants are very sleek-looking adults who frequently show their teeth. They are known for their eagerness in swallowing kids, teachers, even entire classrooms, and transforming them into demonstrations. (Demonstrations, Dear Reader, are model lessons.)

The shark thrashed about, and Mrs. Primrose thought it was because it had lost its budget proposal, but when it aimed itself toward the wading pool, she realized her mistake and ran for the school building, where she called the district office. They sent down two *real* consultants, who advised Mrs. Primrose to stay calm; the shark would fit in nicely with the new science program which would be distributed shortly to all teachers. Lulu was loaded onto a stretcher and driven to a high school swimming pool.

As for Mr. Heather, he was so intent on devouring the pudding, he never realized he had been captured.

"Nothing is going right," said Fritzi.

So the kids covered the hole and Mr. Heather with teachers' manuals and supervisors' bulletins and went off to school.

8

Mr. Bullotad's Ordeals

Mr. Bullotad was muscle-bound. He possessed a pitted, bulbous nose, a large jutting belly, and a jeering voice. Kids who didn't grab a towel fast enough from the towel monitor, kids who soaped themselves too long or tried to avoid a shower, kids who tried to get out of games . . . all were slammed into a corner and butted by Mr. Bullotad's hard-as-rock abdomen.

One day, in the shower, Mr. Bullotad had jeered at Skinny's freckles. "You got the pox, son?"

Skinny hadn't forgotten those words. He was going to get even. He fashioned a belt for himself: a belt resembling a dog's studded collar. The studs were carpet tacks, and it was a marvel of craftsmanship, fitting snugly around Skinny's chest under his shirt. He wore it the day Mr. Bullotad attended the last session of his Human Relations class. This class was geared for physical education teachers and art teachers, attempting to "bridge the gap" that some people think exists between the two groups. Mr. Bullotad and Mr. Heather had to involve themselves in all sorts of relating games, like looking at each other and sitting at the same table and calling each other by their first names. Mr. Heather wore a cologne that Mr. Bullotad didn't like; Mr. Bullotad just wore his *own* cologne (eau de himself), that Mr. Heather didn't like. But because relating was a *must* procedure for renewal of teaching certificates, both teachers were forced to "establish rapport." Rapport rapidly faded when Mr. Heather, in a burst of solidarity, suggested to Mr. Bullotad that it would be "splendid" if the gym towels were tie-dyed and batiked.

So, Mr. Bullotad was in a foul mood. His huge paunch was bowling kids over right and left in gym class. Then Skinny arrived. Late. In the midst of all the kids undressing, Skinny waited, stolid and silent, in his clothes.

Mr. Bullotad paused. His face made the kids shudder. "Malinky! Late again!"

Skinny gazed at Mr. Bullotad without flinching.

"Malinky! Strip!"

Skinny didn't move a muscle.

"Did you *hear* me? I said *strip!*"

"You strip, Mr. Underarms," said Skinny, in a voice that carried to every kid in the room. "I'd like to see that laundry basket of blubber."

Mr. Bullotad's chin snapped up so fast his bones cracked. He started moving towards Skinny, breathing in puffy grunts.

Like an eel, Skinny darted away, taunting: "C'mon, Wet Pits! Let's see ya move that fat!" He grabbed a towel and did a marvelous imitation of a bullfighter. "Toro! Toro!" he shouted.

The kids lined the wall, grinning from ear to ear.

The gym teacher dashed to the door, locked it, and turned again to Skinny, a look of triumph on his face.

"I'll get you!"

The chase went on for three delicious minutes as Skinny waved a towel before Mr. B.'s scarlet face.

Then Skinny fell!

He got to his feet just as Mr. Bullotad reached him.

Skinny pushed out his chest and faced the fleshy battering ram.

Uttering a terrible howl, Mr. Bullotad staggered back. His abdomen had met Skinny's belt.

Snatching up the key ring from where it had fallen on the floor, Skinny opened the door and fled.

Scratchland School was in an uproar. Every day it got worse. One day the kids would be cooperative, the next they would be monsters. It did no good for teachers to lock their doors, because the kids always found keys.

The same things were happening in other schools. The numbers of teachers out on sick leave rose sharply, and it became impossible to find enough substitutes. Teacher-transfer forms piled up higher and higher on administrators' desks.

All teachers were required to take a special new class in the Art of Defending Oneself Against Kids. Mr. Bullotad composed (with the ghostwriting skills of Mr. Snockadocka) a small textbook for teachers on *Punitive Measures*.

The kids retaliated. One afternoon Mr. Bullotad was seated at his desk, counting a number of small white objects.

"What's he doing, Skinny? Can you tell?" asked Curly in a whisper.

"Looks like pieces of soap to me," whispered Skinny. "Now he's puttin' 'em all together to make one big piece . . . and puttin' it in his pocket."

After pocketing the soap, Mr. Bullotad rose and went over to a mirror, where he stood for a few minutes, admiring himself. Suddenly, Big Alice loomed behind him in the mirror.

Mr. Bullotad went dead white. Then he backed off. Big Alice slowly advanced.

There was nowhere for Mr. Bullotad to go but farther into the locker room, until Big Alice, making peculiar and unfriendly noises in her throat, succeeded in cornering Mr. Bullotad in the shower room. Big Alice turned on the hot and then the cold water, keeping Mr. Bullotad alternately roasting and freezing.

Once Mr. Bullotad tried to make a run for it, but Big Alice got down on all fours and nipped him so hard he gave up any idea of escaping. He tried bargaining with her. He would make her the star of a filmstrip on *The Jungle as an Open Classroom*; he swore to make her an officer of the Gym Teachers' Association, with honorary swimming and sauna privileges; he even promised to give her all his trophies. But Big Alice turned a deaf—and bristly—ear.

After the shower, Big Alice demanded some cartwheels and somersaults. Mr. Bullotad stumbled and fumbled through them.

At some period in the past, during the times that Big Alice was given the privilege of participating in human, cultural affairs, she had been exposed to an Appreciation course. That experience had left an indelible mark on her mind.

"Na-chin-skee! Na-chin-skee!" she abruptly began to yell.

Mr. Bullotad was red as a beet and gulping great breaths of air. "What? What?" Mr. B. gasped. He was ready to collapse. "Na-chin-skee *what?*"

"Na-chin-skee! *Do Na-chin-skee!*"

"Oh my God!" cried Mr. Bullotad. "I never *saw* Nijinsky!"

"Na-chin-skee! *Do* Na-chin-skee!" continued Big Alice, moving closer.

"I never saw him, I tell you!" screamed Mr. Bullotad, tears in his eyes.

Big Alice opened her mouth and displayed her canines.

Mr. Bullotad executed a beautiful entrechat.

Then Big Alice had Mr. Bullotad doing push-ups on the trampoline. When he reached twenty-nine, Skinny and Curly came in and made her stop.

Big Alice reluctantly obeyed, and asked if she might eat him.

Skinny said no, it would set a bad example. There might not be any stopping Big Alice once she started *that* sort of thing. If she ate all the teachers, there wouldn't be any war.

9

Mrs. Jerome's Dream
and How It Ended

Things were suddenly quiet at Scratchland. Mr. Snockadocka had resigned and accepted the Trumbull Stickney Chair at the Glossolalia School of Business and Performing Arts in the Petrified Forest. Old Mrs. Solemnsides was attending the J. Edgar Prime Mover Obedience School with her dog, Snitch. Mr. Bullotad sat in his locked office writing a novel about a heroic gym teacher who battles a wild interplanetary creature that emerges from a shower head to threaten the world. Mrs. Jerome continued to plan the training of Big Alice. Dr. Pucker and Colonel Kratz were creating committees, signing Declarations of Principle, and writing memos.

The Scratchland kids were vanishing. Hundreds of kids had defected from schools everywhere, and no one seemed to notice.

Mrs. Jerome did notice that Big Alice was gone. She missed her.

Big Alice had found an excellent hideout, high on a hill, in a new sixteen-unit apartment building. The units were all vacant because its owner had gone bankrupt and lost it to the bank. The bank, in turn, had decided to raze the apartment house and build a new parking lot. It remained standing because the wrecking crew was involved in union negotiations.

Big Alice enjoyed skulking about the units watching cracks form in the plaster, shingles loosen and fall off the roof, doors warp, and walls stain with damp and mildew. At night she toured the trash cans in the neighborhood. She devoured any meaty tidbits she found—half-chewed spareribs, unfinished chicken bones, and the like. Dogs and cats gave her a wide berth.

Mrs. Jerome sensed that Big Alice was somewhere near Scratchland, and took to walking about the school grounds late at night. Armed with her old college text, *The Socio-Physiological Foundations of Educational Stability and Determinate Motivation with Application to Stenotypy,* and a large, moist soup bone, Mrs. Jerome roamed the neighborhood.

Alice watched. The odor from the soup bone made her eyebrows bristle and her nose twitch. It was the book Mrs. Jerome carried that stopped Big Alice from accosting the teacher. It exuded an odor, a malignant and dreary odor, full of danger.

It was inevitable that Big Alice would grow careless. One night, with her head half buried in the remains of a TV dinner, Big Alice was caught off guard. Although Mrs. Jerome was only one person, Big Alice felt surrounded.

"Why, Big Alice! It's you!" cried Mrs. Jerome. "What a surprise! I was so hoping," and she waved her book in the air, "that we could read Chapter Two, 'Roads to Agreement,' together."

Big Alice froze. She had eyes only for the soup bone.

"Come, dear," continued Mrs. Jerome, attempting to take Big Alice's pawlike hand. "I *care,* I really do." She opened the book to the chapter entitled "Language Builds Understanding of Human Relations."

Mrs. Jerome sat on the curbstone, drawing Big Alice down beside her. "We do miss you terribly at Scratchland," she said.

At this point, Big Alice could restrain herself no longer. She grabbed the soup bone and devoured it, bag and all.

"Do you know, Alice, your impulsiveness can be redirected? Please believe this." Mrs. Jerome searched the page, looking for a particular paragraph, but as she did so, Big Alice sank her teeth into Mrs. Jerome's right leg.

"Now, Alice," remonstrated Mrs. Jerome, holding her breath and remembering Professor Weisburd's admonition that Poise Under Pressure Makes Communication Fresher, "let's talk about your hostility."

Big Alice made a face. After swallowing, she sank her teeth into Mrs. Jerome's left leg.

Mrs. Jerome uttered a short, pained cry and tried a new tack. "Alice dear, I do know how fond you are of singing. We shall sing songs from various countries to provide an outlet for your emotions."

Big Alice nodded. Her mouth was full and she could not sing. Mrs. Jerome could, and she did.

Big Alice blinked. She had sniffed the tantalizing odor of lamb chops in the air. She turned away, still chewing.

"Please don't go, Alice," cried Mrs. Jerome. "I know I am reaching you! Just give us a chance, dear! The results of research show us that pupil scores on many standardized tests can be improved dramatically by . . ."

Big Alice wavered. Should she go after the lamb chops or continue with Mrs. Jerome? Big Alice decided to forego the lamb chops. She turned once again to Mrs. Jerome, who still had plenty to say. Mrs. Jerome's mouth remained moving long after the rest of her had vanished.

10

The Remarkable
Mr. Foreclosure

Dr. Pucker and Colonel Kratz were writing memos. They were interrupted by a knock at the office door. It opened, and they faced a slim-looking man in a black jump suit. The man carried a satchel in one hand and a briefcase in the other.

Colonel Kratz, who seemed to know him, waved him in. "Vance, this is Sterling Guts, Mr. Foreclosure's first private secretary."

Sterling Guts nodded.

"How is Mr. Foreclosure?" asked Colonel Kratz.

"Excellent, excellent," replied Sterling Guts, putting down the briefcase and patting the satchel.

Colonel Kratz explained to Dr. Pucker, "Sterling, here, is Mr. Foreclosure's protector and closest friend." He lowered his voice. "Only four people in the world know that Mr. Foreclosure is a mutation—his mother, his father, Sterling Guts, and myself." Pause. "You are number five."

"I am honored," replied Dr. Pucker.

"Mr. Foreclosure decided to admit you into this most closely guarded secret." Sterling Guts indicated the satchel in his right hand. "Mr. Foreclosure, being quite small, never discloses himself to the public, or even to his best friends. He has influential enemies in the world of finance who would not hesitate to ruin him."

"A mutation, you say?" exclaimed Dr. Pucker, staring at the satchel.

"Yes," answered Sterling Guts. "But I need not commend to you, Dr. Pucker, Mr. Foreclosure's great and incisive mind."

"You certainly need not," cried Dr. Pucker. "All the world has heard of Mr. Foreclosure. Nations tremble and governments topple if he but nods his head. But I must say, I've often wondered why he has never been photographed."

"Now, sir, you shall find out," said Sterling Guts, placing the satchel on a table and unzipping it. Inside was a miniature mansion, no larger than a footstool. Sterling Guts set it on Dr. Pucker's desk.

"He'll be out in a moment," said Colonel Kratz. "It takes him awhile to get from the top floor to the front entrance."

After two minutes of excruciatingly tense waiting, Dr. Pucker stood up. "I've seen no one come in or out. What is this, a hoax?"

Suddenly, the tiny door opened and a large red ant came out.

Dr. Pucker's face grew crimson. "Well, gentlemen! Where is your Mr. Foreclosure?"

"There he is, sir," said Sterling Guts. "And well prepared, as usual. He has his brief under one mandible."

Colonel Kratz leaned over to Dr. Pucker and in a whisper said: "Mr. Foreclosure is a red ant."

There appeared to be nothing human about Mr. Foreclosure. He had an unusually large head with fierce-looking jaws and long antennae. The tail end of his body bore a wicked stinger. He stood erect on two of his six legs and gazed up at Dr. Pucker.

Dr. Pucker felt a shiver go down his back; the palms of his hands grew cold and moist.

Sterling Guts placed his hand before Mr. Foreclosure, and the ant crawled on it. "Mr. Foreclosure," declared Guts proudly, "speaks fourteen languages. He has been educated in the best schools."

"In the best schools?" the principal murmured.

"Yes," responded Colonel Kratz in another whisper. "In someone's pocket, of course."

Sterling Guts laid his hand on the principal's shoulder. Dr. Pucker shuddered as the ant crawled up and perched on the lobe of his ear. The principal controlled a wild desire to swat the insect.

Mr. Foreclosure cupped two of his mandibles and in a tiny, sandpapery voice (in perfect English) said: "My agents have been observing you for three years, Dr. Pucker. Your struggle against continual harassment by kids has been admirable."

Dr. Pucker gulped. "Thank you, sir! Thank you!"

"We have enlisted you in our plan to defeat the Kids once and for all. You are now a member of our team."

Dr. Pucker gulped again. "Oh, thank you, sir! I shall try to be worthy of this honor, I assure you!"

"Now sit, sir, and allow me to travel to your knee, where it will be easier for you to see me."

Dr. Pucker carefully sat down and waited. He was sweating. Soon, the red ant appeared on his knee.

Mr. Foreclosure chuckled. "You need not have been so careful, Dr. Pucker. I am very good at hanging on to objects and am not easily shaken off." This remark made the principal shiver again. "There is no reason to suppose," continued Mr. Foreclosure, "that the kids will let bygones be bygones. Their short memories are treacherous and vindictive. I have long suffered from the indignities of the young."

"Yes," replied Dr. Pucker, "I remember reading about what the kids in Nova Scotia did to your lovely home, your lovely factory, your lovely bank, and your *lovely* insurance company. Simply disgraceful!"

Like all ants, Mr. Foreclosure had two kinds of eyes, simple and compound. A stern and relentless expression flickered in them both. "I sit," he said, "as chairman of Scratchland's School Board and a trustee on the Boards of nine hundred and eighty-three other institutions. I am well aware of the nature of this problem. What is most alarming is that kids are *organizing*. Like Scratchland's Skinny Malinky and his cronies, kids everywhere are preparing themselves for what looks like a major war." Mr. Foreclosure paused and blinked his red eyes. "Now, gentlemen, it would be easy for me to withdraw and allow the proper school authorities to handle this, but I see this as a personal challenge. I will not stand by and see the kids destroy our educational institutions and devour our teachers."

Colonel Kratz's face grew grim. "You mean, sir, the episode concerning Mrs. Jerome?"

"I do. I cannot think of a more disrespectful act than a kid devouring a teacher. That behavior *will not be tolerated!*"

"It's all-out war," said Colonel Kratz in a low voice.

"It is indeed," replied Mr. Foreclosure. "We have in Mr. Guts here"—Mr. Foreclosure glanced affectionately at his first secretary—"a superb strategist. He has been following the Kids' movement from the very outset and has been working very closely with the International PTA." Wriggling his antennae, Mr. Foreclosure gestured towards Guts. "Sterling, tell our friends our plans."

Sterling Guts took a breath. "The International PTA, over which Mr. Foreclosure presides as ex officio president, treasurer, and legal counsel, announced in a secret memorandum last night that it has completed Project Metamorphosis."

"Wonderful!" cried Colonel Kratz.

"What is Project Metamorphosis?" asked Dr. Pucker.

"It's our code name for the Status Quo Solidifier," replied the Colonel, lowering his voice. "The Foreclosure Institute has been working on it for seven years."

"Eighteen million dollars of my own personal fortune has gone into perfecting the Solidifier," declared Mr. Foreclosure.

"I am ashamed to say I have never heard of it," exclaimed the principal.

"Top secret," explained Sterling Guts. "For seven years, Dr. Kuzma Kockamoon, the greatest science teacher in the world, has experimented with a practical device that could harness the enormous power of peanut butter."

"Peanut butter?" said Dr. Pucker.

"That's right," replied Guts. "Two weeks ago, Dr. Kockamoon split the peanut butter atom. It is now possible to build a machine in which we will be able to change Kids into Young People: the Status Quo Solidifier."

"Oh my!" exclaimed Dr. Pucker.

"Through the use of the Status Quo Solidifier, we will be able to isolate kidness in a kid and redirect it."

"Oh my!" was all Dr. Pucker could say.

"It is the ultimate weapon," remarked Mr. Foreclosure, grooming his antennae on his forelegs. "The Kids' War will be completely smashed!"

There was silence until Mr. Foreclosure, raising a warning feeler, said, "Nevertheless, gentlemen, it is a race for time. We must hold the Kids off until we are fully in possession of this weapon, the first model of which is being rushed into production even now, as we talk."

Before anyone could comment on this, a small sound, very much like the squeak of a mouse, was heard.

"That's my phone," exclaimed Mr. Foreclosure, and he skittered inside his mansion. After several minutes, he emerged, his compound eyes shiny with anger. "The news is indeed bad, my friends. The Kids are on the march. There are uprisings everywhere. A large army is now, at this very moment, marching toward Scratchland! We haven't a minute to lose!"

11

A Last Warning

Barley Chops was born ugly and he stayed ugly. Even as a baby, his features were too large to be cute and too uneven to be called interesting. As he grew, Barley's hands and feet outstripped the rest of him. Barley came from a family with small hands and feet and tiny, straight noses. He came from a family of teachers, but Barley was a nonreader and nonwriter. When he was ten, his parents sent him to vocational school, and though Barley displayed marked talent in working with his large hands, he displayed none at all in getting along with teachers. In despair and with relief, Barley's parents sent him to a work-therapy camp—first one, then another, then a third. Then, a last chance. The last chance was not, as any kid knows, a last chance at all, but a chain, and Barley, in due time, snapped it loose and fled.

For months, Barley had lived in various junk and salvage yards, feeling sorry for himself and angry at everyone else. There the news that a kid named Skinny Malinky had started a war against teachers changed Barley. He invented a communications system that linked kids living in junkyards all over the country. These were kids with grease on their hands, whose brains were as inflammable as oil-soaked rags, kids who hated school. They lived in scrap-metal mountains, towed-away junkers, abandoned tenements, in waste-yards and pits filled with crumpled papers from school wastebaskets. The Kids rose like scraps, like the nuts and bolts of some discarded machine, and marched with Barley Chops. They joined Skinny Malinky and the Mosquitoes near Scratchland.

The new contingent was a welcome addition. They were tough and disciplined. Skinny gave Barley a seat equal to his in the War Council. Barley respected Skinny and listened to him. Skinny, for his part, thought Barley was a mechanical wizard and told him so.

The Kids' army expanded rapidly. Besides Skinny and his allies, there were kids who had been living beneath bleachers in ball parks and in X-rated movie houses. The ranks swelled hourly with kids from wilderness areas, national parks, and wild bird sanctuaries. They came on foot, on bikes, roller skates, and motorcycles. They all had heard about Skinny Malinky and the War and they wanted to take part. A massive confrontation was going to take place, and it would happen at Scratchland School.

Mr. Foreclosure was not idle. A large contingent of teachers, all strict taskmasters from Eastern Fundamental Schools (where kids learned their *basics*), was flying to Scratchland in a fleet of Mr. Foreclosure's own jets. Special Services teachers with credentials in Cultural Retribution and advanced degrees in Intellectual Dismemberment were recruited along with a hard core of handpicked, supervisory disciplinarians. All these people had the distinct advantage of having always been adults. They had learned to read and write when only months old, and by six years of age were earning salaries in prosperous businesses. The important thing about these people was that by six they were all *solvent*. Mr. Foreclosure had great faith in them.

Dr. Pucker trained his powerful binoculars on the forest of tents beyond the playground. The air was black with the smoke from dozens of campfires. "Fantastic!" he murmured. "I never would have believed it." He, Colonel Kratz, Sterling Guts, and Mr. Foreclosure (hidden beneath one of Guts's lapels) had turned the principal's office into a War Room. TV monitors, newly installed radar, a table filled with a dozen red telephones, and on the walls, many large maps with orange and black pins in them lent a martial air to the room. The telephones never stopped ringing, telegrams were constantly being slid under the door, and the *blip! blip!* of the radar sounded as a low-key counterpoint.

"The helicopter has arrived! asserted Colonel Kratz, hanging up a phone receiver.

"You mean—Project Metamorphosis?" asked Dr. Pucker, his face turning pink.

Sterling Guts ran out the door, to the helicopter on the playground. Beside it stood old Mrs. Solemnsides and her Peke dog Snitch. Between the dog's jaws was an envelope. Guts took old Mrs. Solemnsides's hand in his and squeezed it. Because she had been Mr. Foreclosure's father's elocution teacher and highly regarded by his family, she had been selected to accompany the secret weapon on its trip from the nation's capital to Scratchland.

"I can't tell you how pleased and proud we are of you, ma'am!" said Sterling Guts.

"Thank you, sonny! That's very sweet of you!" replied the old woman, beaming. She handed Guts the envelope. "Here are the instructions. It has to be assembled."

Guts tore open the official seal and drew out a sheaf of papers. He shouted to the teachers who had gathered around the helicopter, "It's the Status Quo Solidifier, gentlemen!"

Cries of pleasure came from every window of Scratchland.

"What will it do?" asked Dr. Pucker in a quiet voice.

77

Sterling Guts smiled a bit pompously. "It can age a kid in less than ten seconds, giving him his first gray hair, and inducing a more conservative outlook in his nature."

A loud "Ah!" rose from everyone's throats. There was clapping.

Guts cleared his throat. "Now we must act."

Skinny, Curly, Fritzi, and Barley were sitting in Barley's tent when a voice like thunder blasted their ears.

"Now hear this! Now hear this!"

Kids rushed out of their tents in silent groups, looked up into the sky, and listened.

"Kids, this is your *last chance*. I repeat, *This is your last chance*. Go back to your classrooms. Surrender to your teachers. You will not be required to bring a note from home. Your absence will be excused. I repeat, your absence will be excused. You have twenty-four hours in which to return to school. If you do not return by this time tomorrow, we will come and get you."

The kids began to boo and hiss.

"We have a weapon," boomed the voice.

The kids swiftly quieted.

"We have in our possession a weapon which will subdue all kids forever. It is the result of Project Metamorphosis and it is called the Status Quo Solidifier. I repeat: It is the Status Quo Solidifier. If you do not surrender, we have no option but to use the Solidifier. The choice is yours."

This time there was little booing. Kids milled around and talked in hushed voices.

"We're gonna have to answer 'em, Skinny," said Barley, scratching his scalp and watching the dandruff fall.

"We have to answer to our own troops first," replied Fritzi, who had gotten herself a uniform. Across her chest hung several medals and ribbons, one of which said: 37TH ANNUAL REUNION 10TH NEW YORK CAVALRY VETERAN ASSOCIATION BUFFALO N.Y. OCTOBER 18, 1898.

Skinny was worried. "What do you think, Curly?"

"Oh, tumultuous triceratops, teachers have been talking about that Project Metamorphosis for years! I think it's a bluff!"

Barley rubbed his chin, where a skimpy tuft of hair had recently shown itself. "Mebbe. Mebbe not." His large gray eyes focused inward. "Have you noticed that man, Skinny, near the school office? In the black jump suit?"

"Yes. He looks like a weasel. Who is he?"

Barley sighed. "He's Sterling Guts. Number Two man in Mr. Foreclosure's organization."

"Who's Mr. Foreclosure, anyway?" asked Curly.

"I've heard of him," said Fritzi. "He's one of those millionaires sticking his nose into everything. He makes lots of noise about how kids should act."

"He's chairman of the School Board and he's kids' worst enemy," said Barley. "I ought to know. My parents shipped me to a camp run by the Foreclosure Foundation. I saw Guts there several times."

"What was it like?" Skinny asked. Curly's thumb popped into his mouth.

"We were guinea pigs. They used us to test spinach-leaf cigarettes. Mr. Foreclosure owns just about all the cigarette factories. He wanted to launch a new cigarette because not enough people were buying his other cigarettes. We had to smoke a pack a day, for thirty days."

"Wow!" cried Fritzi. "Ugh!"

"Then it was soap," said Barley. "Which one of Mr. Foreclosure's soaps cleaned the least? That was the soap they wanted to sell the most. I took baths six times a day."

Groans from everyone.

Skinny paced and bit his lip.

Fritzi was unpinning her medals. One by one, she blew on them and polished them on her pants leg. Then she repinned them.

Curly's eyebrows met in a little hill over his nose. Thumb in his mouth, he asked: "Wash thith Focloshure like, Barley?"

"Never seen him. Not many people have. He lives at Lake Cachuma. He's a mysterious guy."

"Skinny, are you worried about that Status Quo whatchamajigger?" asked Fritzi, who had all her medals back in place.

Skinny stopped and brushed the orange hair away from his eyes. "I guess I am." He squatted and looked at each of his friends. "Is it dumb to go on?"

"Skinny!" Fritzi cried and squatted down next to him. "Dumb? How can you say that?"

"This is the biggest war Kids have ever made against Teachers, Skinny," added Curly, waving his wet thumb in the air. "And it's because of you."

Barley squatted too and laid his large, rough hand on Skinny's shoulder. "I know what's bothering you, Skinny. You think we're taking an awful chance—in case there really is a Solidifier—right?"

Skinny grimaced. "I hate to be the one, Barley, to . . . to get kids put into that thing."

Barley scowled. "I don't trust 'em. They'd put us in it anyway, whether we surrender or not."

"Right," said Fritzi. "Mr. Foreclosure and the Teachers aren't going to pass up a chance like that. We've got to fight. No other choice."

"I agree," piped up Curly. "Indubitably. Can't turn back now."

"Okay," Skinny said.

12

Skinny's Dream

That night, Skinny dreamed he stood in the doorway of a school office that stretched for miles. There were rows of desks receding into the distance. Mountainous wastebaskets loomed in the corners.

Ida stood in the center of the huge room. Her black skin glowed and she was beautiful. She was wringing a mop over a bucket.

"Look, Ida," Skinny said, "they've taken away my freckles."

Ida dropped her mop, put her hands on his shoulders, and slowly turned him around. "You just whiter'n a sheet, Skinny. Your head look on fire."

"What'll I do, Ida?"

"They take away what's you, and that's all you got. And that's bad." Some kind of coat materialized in Ida's arms, and she tossed it to him. "Wear this."

"What is it, Ida?" he said and wrapped himself in it. It was wonderfully cool.

"It's old-time freckles I saved. Been sewing 'em together. I just got enough for one coat. And you can have it."

"Thanks, Ida." But Skinny had trouble covering himself. The coat was shrinking, and it had no sleeves.

"Whose freckles were these, Ida?"

"I don't know. I found 'em in teachers' drawers. Locked away."

Then Skinny found himself covered with fur, and he stroked his arms. The fur was russet and stood on end.

Ida turned away and began mopping the floor.

Skinny, arms outstretched, began running. Then he glided up from the floor, and in a moment he was lazily circling a wastebasket which opened up beneath him like the crater of an extinct volcano.

"Lots of paper in this wastebasket, Ida. Can I dump it for you?"

"No, don't touch it. Too many kids in there."

And Skinny saw that Ida was right. The crumpled papers were all kids, and they gazed up at Skinny so piteously that he wanted to cry.

"Please, Ida, can I dump it for you?"

Ida's brows knitted. "No! They're safe there."

Skinny flew over another wastebasket, filled with creatures bent into odd shapes, hands clawing upwards.

"Don't dump that one neither, Skinny Malinky! Don't dump those teachers on my clean floor! I don't want 'em out here writin' ree-ports about you and me!"

Skinny felt himself falling, and he flattened into a piece of paper on a desk blotter.

Ida's huge eyes bore down on him. "Where you hiding from me, Skinny? You tell me."

"I'm here, Ida, inside these words."

Ida lifted up the paper, reading it carefully. "Don't see you. Which words?"

Large capital letters, *D*'s and *F*'s, turned black and bold against the white page.

"Here I am, Ida," the letters said and danced up into Ida's sober face. She whisked them away with an impatient gesture.

"That's not you, Skinny. Them are report-card fruit flies. Live in teachers' handwritin'."

Then Skinny was himself again, sitting behind a desk.

His body was speckled with handwritten *D*'s and *F*'s. "What do you think of my *new* freckles, Ida?"

"That's just teacher paint. It come off in soap and water. You more than writing, Skinny."

"No, I'm not, Ida." Skinny's voice wobbled and he was holding himself tightly so he wouldn't lose control. "Who wrote my freckles, Ida?"

"It's all the words you licked off the wall, Skinny." Ida's voice came from the top of the room. She was upside down on the ceiling, mopping it on her hands and knees.

Ida shook some drops down on him. "Skinny," she said in her most serious voice.

"What, Ida?"

"You still got my luck rabbit?"

"Sure. Sure I do." And Skinny reached into his pocket—but it was gone! Frantically, he turned all his pockets inside out, shook himself, while Ida's sorrowing eyes got larger and larger.

He woke. It was dawn. His hand scrabbled into his pocket, found the rabbit, and held it tightly. Then he examined his arms. His freckles were still with him, but a deep sense of foreboding grew in him, and he began to tremble.

13

Big Alice's Finest Hour

After her "learning experience" with Mrs. Jerome, Big Alice retired into her favorite trash can, curled herself into a ball, and went to sleep. For three days and three nights, she slept, never moving a muscle. Her trash can stood on top of the hill, beside the apartment house overlooking Scratchland School.

On the fourth day, Big Alice woke and pushed the lid off with her head. There below her was the Kids' army, spread out as far as she could see. There were small tents and large tents. There were lean-tos and sheds, all kinds of ingenious shelters that kids had thrown up around the school. Many tents were painted with brightly colored insignia and sayings. Skinny Malinky's tent had a picture on it of a kid with a drawn and bloody blackboard pointer standing over the inert body of a well-known teacher. The kids from national parks had drawn animals, some of which resembled certain principals. Barley Chops's tent was covered with strange equations worked into designs. Banners and flags flew everywhere. Some were made from business suits and white dress shirts; others were from desk blotters, reading charts, kindergarten paintings, and gym towels. Teachers' neckties were strung from yardsticks stuck in the ground.

Everywhere there were kids, milling around, roasting wieners and marshmallows, telling sad stories about teachers, about classes, about the schools that had expelled them. Those kids who had never flunked a class or been expelled remained quiet, embarrassed. Many kids were worried. Rumors flew fast and thick, many concerning Mr. Foreclosure. Some kids said he was a devil; others believed he could turn himself invisible at will. It was a time of nervous joy and deep fear.

As Big Alice stared down at the Kids' camp, she was reminded of an illustration in a book. Yes. Tents . . . and banners . . . and two figures in an open field. Big Alice slavered and made guttural noises and got down on her knees and paced. An idea was forming in her head. It became larger and larger. This war of Kids against Teachers was *her* war. The conflict, in a very special and private way, belonged to *her*. And since it was hers, it was up to her to resolve it.

Poor Big Alice! She had lost the instinctive awareness of danger learned in the Lake Cachuma Wildlife Preserve. It churned in her bloodstream, but she didn't feel it. The hairs on her bony wrists stood on end, and she howled a long, beautiful howl. Then, throwing caution to the wind, she bounded down the hill just as Skinny, Curly, Fritzi, and Barley trudged back to their tent from a meeting.

"I think we should go ahead and attack now," said Barley. "We outnumber 'em at least ten to one."

Curly interrupted. "We're definitely soo-perior in numbers, but—"

"But what?" said Skinny testily.

"Maybe it doesn't matter."

"What doesn't matter?" asked Barley, but he and Skinny knew what Curly was thinking. Did the teachers really possess that terrible secret weapon? And would they use it?

"I was surprised at how many kids wanted to ask for a truce," said Fritzi, lifting the tent flap. The boys followed her inside the tent.

"Not as many as wanted to attack," said Barley. "They're scared, that's what!"

Skinny scratched himself in several places and examined his fingers. There were no more nails to bite.

"The kids want action and want it *now*," rasped Barley, spitting towards a corner. "They won't wait much longer!"

The tent flap opened and Big Alice stood there. Eyes wild, she half yelled, half moaned, "Ar-tha! Ar-tha!"

"What's she mean, Curly?" asked Skinny.

Curly, puzzled, shook his head and tried to pat Big Alice. "Whaddaya mean, 'Ar-tha'? I don't get it."

Big Alice shook his hand off her arm. *"Er-ment! Er-ment! Ar-tha! Ar-tha!"* From her pocket she took the remains of a lamb chop, the bone picked clean. She held it high in the air and then threw it violently down to the ground. *"Ar-tha! Er-ment! Er-ment! King Ar-tha!"*

The kids stared at her and then at one another.

Fritzi kicked at the bone.

Big Alice snatched it up and threw it down again, repeating the same words.

Fritzi jumped up. "I've got it!" She turned to Big Alice. "King Arthur? King Arthur?"

Big Alice nodded several times, her golden eyes shining.

"Tournament?" Fritzi tried. "Tournament?"

Big Alice picked up the bone and dashed it to the ground again, uttering throaty sounds of pleasure and bobbing her head.

Skinny bit off a large piece of skin on his index finger. "Tournament?" he said. "You mean, she wants a *tournament?*"

"She wants to challenge the teachers to a tournament," declared Fritzi. "Like King Arthur."

"Where did *she* ever hear about King Arthur?" exclaimed Barley.

Big Alice shot a venomous look at him.

"She wants to throw down her bone, I mean, glove," explained Fritzi, looking at Big Alice with new appreciation. "How about that!"

Skinny drew Fritzi aside. "Why is she talking so bad?" he whispered. "She can talk better 'n that."

"She's reverting to her animal state," responded Fritzi. "She does it when she's excited about something." She gazed in admiration at Big Alice. "She wants the teachers to pick a champion to fight her. Whoever wins, wins the War."

Big Alice nodded vigorously.

The kids were quiet. Fritzi, Curly, and Barley Chops liked the idea of a tournament, but, noticing Skinny's serious face, they waited for him to speak.

Skinny's freckles turned a deep red. A sense of fear rose from his stomach. He pushed it down as hard as he could. "I know you're tough, Big Alice, but I think the War is bigger than one fight."

Big Alice looked sullen.

"How can you say that, Skinny, to the classiest idea yet?" said Curly.

"Yeah!" echoed Barley.

Big Alice looked from one kid to another.

After a long silence, Skinny said, "Do you really think the teachers would agree to a tournament? And what if they don't?"

"If they *don't* agree, then we attack tonight! Either way, we win!" cried Barley, slapping Curly on the back so heartily that Curly's thumb was jerked out of his mouth.

"In-*dub*-it-ably!" said Curly, kicking at him.

"We'll have a general meeting, Curly," said Skinny. "Barley, help us get the kids together."

The Kids assembled on the Scratchland playing field. When they heard Big Alice's idea, they whooped and hollered and cheered for a full minute. They voted overwhelmingly for a tourney. The handful of kids who voted against it were resoundingly booed and hissed.

Two hours later, the Kids stood massed before their tents, facing Scratchland School.

Holding a stick with a white shirt flying from it, Skinny advanced slowly towards the school. When he was within twenty yards of the door, he stopped and waited. Soon the door opened and Dr. Pucker stepped out, a grim expression on his face.

The crowd of kids parted to let Big Alice lope through. She came up to Skinny, smiled, and got up on her hind legs. She held the lamb chop bone with a note rolled around it. She threw it at Dr. Pucker's feet. As the principal picked up the bone, Big Alice lifted her head and laughed a Grade A hyena laugh. There was no one, kid or teacher, who didn't feel his flesh creep.

Dr. Pucker unfolded the paper and read it, grimacing. "What's this all about, Skinny Malinky?" he said, in a cold and cautious voice.

"It's Big Alice's challenge. Accept it and you have a fair, fighting chance to win the War. If you don't take it—*look out!*"

Skinny and Big Alice turned around and walked back to the crowd. Dr. Pucker, lips set, quickly retreated inside the school with the lamb chop bone between his fingertips.

The principal, Colonel Kratz, old Mrs. Solemnsides, Snitch, and Sterling Guts (with Mr. Foreclosure listening from under his lapel) held a Council of War in Dr. Pucker's office.

"It's a stroke of luck," remarked Sterling Guts. "The kids have played right into our hands."

"How can you say that?" declared Dr. Pucker. "There isn't a teacher in the world who can hold his own against that monstrous girl!"

"The tournament gives us time, time to assemble the

Status Quo Solidifier. Isn't that so, Sterling?" asked Colonel Kratz.

"Exactly! Let the kids make the rules for the tournament. We shall make a few rules of our own." Guts pretended to straighten the carnation in his lapel as he bent his head and listened to the soft words of Mr. Foreclosure.

"Well, who's to be *our* champ-een?" screeched Mrs. Solemnsides.

"Never fear, dear Mrs. Solemnsides," soothed Guts. "We shall work it out."

"Then you believe, Sterling, that we should go ahead with the tournament?" asked Colonel Kratz.

"Mr. Foreclosure wants it that way," answered Sterling Guts. "And I have no doubt as to the outcome."

14

The Tournament

An hour after Big Alice made her challenge, the Teachers accepted it.

Under a flag of truce, a committee met to plan the tournament. Curly, who had read thousands of books since the age of six, and Barley, because of his mechanical ability, represented the Kids.

The Teachers were represented by Commodore Putsch, a portly man with a glorious walrus mustache from which his fingers rarely strayed. He was a history buff who specialized in the Middle Ages. Mrs. Solemnsides, who had once been Henry the Second in a pageant, was his aide. "The passage of arms," as the Commodore called it, would be laid out in front of Scratchland School.

Preparations began. Half a dozen homes had to be razed to make room for the enclosure, an oval circus, affording a clear view to all spectators. It was fenced except at its northern and southern extremities, where entry for the combatants was accommodated by strong wooden gates. At its northern end, the kids, under the able leadership of Barley Chops, built a mock castle of wood where they planned their strategies. On the castle turret flew Big Alice's standard, a brooding hyena head on a field of daisies.

Opposite the Kids' castle, on the southern tip of the enclosure, stood a replica of the National Alliance of Teacher Cartels Retirement Home and Savings and Loan, which Mr. Foreclosure, sparing no expense, had had constructed by hundreds of jobless minority teachers who worked feverishly around the clock in order to finish the edifice in the two weeks allotted.

The side of the arena where the kids were to sit was decorated with graffiti. The teachers' side was hung with giant poster-portraits of world-famous educators, such as John Immolate Callous the Third and Dr. Ludmilla Rose Horrenda, pioneer of Sit-Still Social Studies kits.

Towards the center and within the arena, or "lists," as Curly insisted on calling it, was built the judges' platform. Sterling Guts and Colonel Kratz would represent the Teachers; Fritzi and Barley Chops would stand for the Kids.

The day of the tournament dawned bright and clear, not too cool, not too warm.

The kids began arriving early, filling up the galleries, some eating, some drinking, all pushing and squabbling, buzzing like a hive of bees.

At nine o'clock the Scratchland School bell rang. The teachers filed into the arena in two straight lines, a man's line and a woman's line. Instantly kids began shouting, hooting, pointing at teachers they recognized. The noise level rose as more teachers entered and took their seats. They wore their very best clothes. The men wore white dress shirts, ties, and three-piece suits. Their shoes shone. The women were in long dresses and they wore Professional Organization pins on their bosoms.

The teachers of younger children sat on small rug squares on the ground. Just above them in the bleachers were the upper-grade teachers, who, once settled, ignored everyone, correcting old papers on their knees. Higher still sat the secondary teachers, with units of study balanced on their laps. On a higher level sat the professors composing instructions for their teaching assistants and proctors.

Highest of all, on what looked like thrones beneath a rich, tapestried canopy, lounged the officers of the Association of Holders of Advanced Degrees. Mrs. Solemnsides served as hostess in a brightly flowered dress which she had worn for her Graduation Ball at Miss Mary's Replenishing School in Basel, Switzerland. It still looked as good as new. Snitch wore a snappy jacket with mother-of-pearl buttons and the blue ribbon he had been awarded at J. Edgar Prime Mover Obedience School.

Finally, when the bleachers were crammed full, the judges filed onto their stand.

Four helicopters now approached the arena. Skinny watched them, his face sober and a finger at his mouth. "I don't like it," he muttered.

The kids' chattering subsided. The teachers looked up from their papers, folded their hands in their laps, and waited.

The judges' platform was shaded by the old elm tree where Curly, Skinny, and Fritzi had held their first, important meeting. Two wooden shields hung from its lowest branch. One shield had the French word *Paix* on it; the other, plated with iron, displayed the word *Guerre*. Both shields, swinging from the branch, now became the focal point of everyone's eyes.

Commodore Putsch, in natty uniform, walked toward the tree holding a gavel in his hand. He stopped, struck with his gavel the shield which said *Paix*, and stood at attention.

A hundred band teachers, ten abreast, bugles in their hands, entered the lists. Their uniforms were new but too small, the shirt sleeves above their wrists, the pants cuffs barely over their shins. The band teachers lifted the instruments to their lips, and a rousing fanfare swept over the crowd. It was well played, and even the kids joined in the applause.

The Commodore marched to the judges' stand. "Most honored and noble judges! Skinny Malinky and his company, henceforth called the Kids, present themselves as challengers, ready to engage the company henceforth known as the Teachers, under the valiant leadership of Dr. Vance Pucker."

He paused. One kid started to boo and was hastily shushed.

The Commodore cleared his throat and resumed: "There shall be four encounters. The first three trials of skill shall be between teams of equal number. The lances will be blunted, the swords pointless, with dulled edges. Those whose lances become splintered and who become unhorsed must leave the field."

Commodore Putsch took out a large silk handkerchief. The kids sat tensely on the edges of their seats, waiting for him to wave it as the signal to begin . . . but the Commodore merely lifted it and blew heartily, one nostril and then the other. Then, with dignity, he walked to the center of the lists, between the two boxes where each leader sat. "The fourth and last passage of arms shall be . . . *to the death.*"

Not a sound could be heard.

"Each side shall present its champion. These two champions, through trial by combat, will resolve the conflicts of this war. The victor shall have the honor of delivering the terms of surrender to the vanquished, who will yield. Unconditionally."

A low humming came from the stands.

"Don't forget my instructions, now, Sterling, for the last combat," murmured Mr. Foreclosure from Guts's tiepin.

"I won't, sir," murmured Guts, placing a finger behind his tie and allowing Mr. Foreclosure to nip it affectionately.

The humming was louder. There appeared behind

the southern and northern barriers a vast company of riders. The kids rose excitedly, as did many teachers. The gates opened, and to the flourish of trumpets, the first, opposing entries rode into the arena.

The Teachers were dressed in gray jogging pants and sweat shirts. They wore coats of mail and thigh protectors of shaped leather. Leather pieces edged in silver were buckled about their arms and elbows, and heavy gauntlets with wide cuffs covered their hands and wrists. Over the hauberks was sewn a coat of arms, which consisted of the letters *SLBP* entwined into crossed yardsticks. These, then, were the Special Learning Behavior Problem teachers. They were helmeted and carried lances.

Advancing toward the teachers was a company of Kids dressed in suits of armor. Because of Curly's meticulous research and Barley Chops's marvelous ability to make things, the armor was superbly crafted. It was modeled after suits made by the great armorers of the fifteenth century. The emblem which waved from the tips of their lances was a kid's face with tongue extended, on a field of broken chalk. The kids wore helmets, and protruding from the open visors were bubbles of gum. This was the Peanut Butter and Jam gang.

As everyone rose and cheered, the Commodore made his way between the two teams, shouting, "Largesse, largesse, gallant company!"

And from the galleries, the stands, the boxes, a shower of candies and gum rained down. (In SLBP classes, these are all rewards for good behavior.)

A single trumpeter blew, and the speech and laughter died away.

Both kids and teachers reined in their horses—sticks with handsome wooden heads, bushy manes, and painted eyes.

"Glory to the brave!" Commodore Putsch declared, and dropped his handkerchief. The two forces began the long gallop to the center of the arena. Four hundred riders swept across the field.

"Death to the SLBP!" cried one kid, who was in the lead.

"Up with the Stanford-Binet!" yelled back a teacher in the stands.

"Up with the Pintner-Cunningham!" echoed another.

Everyone was yelling. The teachers shouted the names of the tests they were qualified to give, which sounded like obscenities to the kids. They responded with the language arts learned on bathroom walls.

Thud! Crash! The two groups collided in a wild jumble of horses, lances, Teachers, and Kids. A good quarter of the horde had been overturned. Riders sprawled on the ground, horses broken, and the squires ran into the field to help them withdraw, collecting broken bits of horse along the way.

One tall SLBP teacher named Siegfried Pink, still astride his horse, created havoc within the ranks of the kids, pushing them off their horses with his lance, slamming them about the shoulders and chest when they refused to fall. The kids in the stands howled with anger. Siegfried Pink was already notorious for his heavy-handed methods in the classroom, and the kids recognized him, yelling, "Pigfeed Stink! Pigfeed Stink! Get him! Get him!"

One kid, riding a horse with a black mane and wearing a crest that pictured a green-toothed mouth above a wastebasket filled with toothbrushes, came up behind Siegfried Pink. He planted the end of his lance in the small of Pink's back.

"Foul!" cried the teachers. They booed, then cheered as Siegfried Pink swung around, maneuvering his horse to face his adversary.

"So it's *you*, is it, Dippy O'Toole? Has anyone rented the room in your head yet, eh? Come on, you blunt-witted, lunk-headed, empty-skulled, subnormal, mentally deficient, unteachable—"

In the judges' stand, Fritzi turned to Guts. "Y'hear what your teacher is saying? He's *unprofessional*. He's disqualified under Rule 14."

"You're right," replied Guts, but he made no move to remove Siegfried Pink.

"—unreachable cretin!" And Siegfried Pink zeroed in on Dippy O'Toole.

Fritzi signaled a squire to bring in Siegfried and bench him, just as Dippy successfully dodged his enemy, forcing him into the fence and splintering his horse, cracking his helmet, and possibly his head. By the time two squires reached Mr. Pink, he had lost his senses, and Fritzi flung down her blackboard pointer—signifying the end of the first engagement.

15

The Tournament,
continued

After several minutes of deliberation, the four judges resumed their seats and the crowd quieted. Then Fritzi and Barley stood, hands out, thumbs up. The Kids had won the first encounter.

As the kids stamped their feet and cheered, Skinny scanned the arena with a pair of binoculars. He gazed long at Sterling Guts in the judges' box. He was troubled by something that he couldn't put his finger on. The cuticles around his index fingers were raw and bleeding.

Again, the trumpet. A new group marched onto the field. It was the Hot Lunch Program Fife and Drum Corps, a hundred and fifty pieces led by six majorettes. School cafeteria cooks wearing white aprons and white caps beat drums painted appetizingly with a hot dog in a bun on one side, and on the other a hamburger patty on a plate, knife and fork crossed beneath. The cooks were older ladies with large biceps and strong chins, and they beat their drums fiercely as they approached the judges' stand. There, they came to a stop and saluted. Applause from the teachers was lukewarm.

Colonel Kratz leaned over the balustrade, trying to make out the Latin inscription on each cook's cap.

"I've forgotten all my Latin, Sterling. Translate for me, please."

"It must be a mistake," answered Guts, training his glasses on the cooks. "It says We Make It Worse."

Colonel Kratz, remembering the last school lunch he had eaten, snorted: "No mistake."

Old Mrs. Solemnsides, gazing down at the majorettes, shrieked with joy: "Why, that's Eliza Overcast! She used to be head cook at Auto-da-Fé Vocational!" Forgetting all sense of decorum, the old lady began waving wildly. "Eliza! Eliza! It's me, Fannie Mae—*Chubby cheeks!* Up here, Eliza!"

The deepening scowls on the faces of Dr. and Mrs. Glyphic, who were sitting beside her, brought old Mrs. Solemnsides to herself again, and she coughed embarrassedly into her lace handkerchief.

Behind the drummers, pedaling on unicycles, came a hundred directors and consultants in Food Education, some of the most illustrious names in School Lunchroom Service. There was Sadie Stiff, who originated Turkey Surprise (turkey dinner without turkey) and Potato Gems (baked potato without potato); and Herbert Sorrells Micklejohn, who developed the Thirty-Second Main Dish (for teachers who have only ten minutes for lunch), which slides out, conveniently, from a machine in the washroom.

These riders, many with P.F. (Processed Food) degrees, wore reinforced breast plates and carried spatulas three feet long, with oak handles.

Coming in the opposite direction was a troop of kids, also on unicycles. These were the Food Wasters, famous for leaving whole meals intact on their cafeteria trays, for tasteless jokes about wieners, for flicking peas at lunch aides, and for preferring starvation to one tiny bite of Golden Glow Pizza.

These kids brandished giant butter knives and salad forks and yelled, "Down with creamed spinach!" and "Death to broccoli!" They wore soup tureens on their heads, and across their chests were tied roasting-pan covers. They received a tremendous ovation from their peers.

"Bon appétit!" shouted Commodore Putsch, and the battle began.

From the outset, the Kids were no match for the wily Cooks, who wielded their spatulas with alacrity and diligence. They maneuvered their unicycles almost as skillfully. In fifteen minutes, all but one kid had been knocked off his unicycle and flipped onto the ground. The survivor was a kid named Shuffles, who had given many teachers on lunchroom duty nervous breakdowns. Shuffles was quickly surrounded by a dozen Food Service people.

The kids in the stands stood, shaking their fists, yelling curses. The teachers seated opposite them were all smiles. Many of them belonged to various lunchroom veterans' organizations.

The Cooks closed in on Shuffles. In an instant he was down, and Sadie Stiff herself was sitting on his stomach spooning large globules of Banana Squash Torte down Shuffle's gagging throat.

The second melee was over.

The custodians moved in to lay out the green carpet of false turf for the third contest. Skinny was chewing his nails, and Barley, who had walked over from the judges' stand, watched him. "This is going to be a tough one, Skinny."

"I know. But it's the last one that counts. How is Big Alice feeling?"

"Fritzi says she's in top form and not to worry. But who do you think the Teachers have picked to fight her?"

"I'm tryin' to think of the toughest teacher I ever had. That was Miss Dinsmore. She could pinch so hard, she stopped your circulation. If she's still around, she'd be a proper one for Big Alice to tangle with."

"Oh yeah. I've seen pictures of her. She's the one who always got the Golden Teacher Award, isn't she?"

"Sure. Year after year. She was *the* Golden Teacher.

Even now, when I meet a kid with a purplish-bluish mark on his arm, I just say, 'Golden Teacher?' And he says, 'Yep!'"

The kids and teachers who had left the stands began trooping back. Many had eaten their lunches in their seats. Some kids had been very responsible about depositing their trash in cans. Others had been very careless, leaving candy bar wrappers and pop bottles wherever they fell. Old lunchroom habits are hard to break.

Most teachers who stayed during the intermission ate out of brown paper bags, each individually tagged with name and school. Few of *these* bags littered the area; most were dropped conscientiously into containers.

"Now what's coming up next, Bumpy?" asked Miss Jenny Dunphy of her twin sister from their place in the stands.

"It's the Substitute Teachers' Association, Blessed Martyr Division. Oh! There they are!"

Forming behind the barrier were the substitute teachers, the pick, the very cream of the most disciplined and uncompromising group of teachers ever to take over a Monday morning class anywhere.

"What are those things they're on, Jenny?"

"Mechanized golf carts. But I can't make out what the Kids are driving."

Miss Bambi shaded her eyes. "They're power mowers, Jenny."

The gates opened; the two opposing forces faced each other. A call of trumpets, and the two groups began moving.

"Heavens! What a noise!" cried Miss Jenny. "What does it say on the teachers' standards, Bumpy?"

"Ummm . . . it says We Came, We Saw, We Did Not Return."

The encounter between the Substitute Teachers and the Kids was extraordinary. The subs in their golf carts knew exactly what they were doing. Very quickly, they encircled the power mowers. Those mowers that escaped the encirclement were ruthlessly trapped by rapid, rearguard action. The kids were stricken. Their machines were larger but clumsier than the golf carts. Some kids handled the mowers expertly—they had been mowing lawns for years—but the golf carts were heavily plated and sustained little or no damage when hit, and they could easily be righted after a collision. The mowers, once overturned, became useless. Kids who left their mowers were rounded up under a sign that read Casualties.

The din was terrific and the smell of fumes was overwhelming. It was an unqualified disaster for the Kids, a complete victory for the Substitute Teachers.

During the wild applause, Miss Jenny turned to her sister and said sotto voce, "I just hope the next round goes better."

Miss Bambi looked around at her cheering colleagues and replied in a low voice, "So do I, dear." And she winked.

16

The Outcome

The field was cleared once again. The clamor from the stands was deafening as Commodore Putsch slowly walked across the lists and stood beneath the elm. The stands grew silent, and the Commodore's voice resounded.

"Between the two champions there shall be trial by combat, on foot, with axes, swords, and daggers. Seven strikes shall be allowed for axes; eleven for swords; fifteen for daggers. If a combatant is struck down and unable to recover his or her feet, his or her squires shall enter the lists and remove him or her. If neither combatant is struck down by the fifteenth stroke of the dagger, then both combatants will be free to devise any possible means to deliver a fatal blow."

A droning came from the spectators. Some teachers were already outlining, in their minds, new Social Studies curricula based on the War Between the Teachers and the Kids.

The sun rolled past its zenith; there was a cloudless sky. Banners and pennants hung limp from their poles. The stadium resembled a great ship becalmed.

And then there was a movement at the northern end

of the enclosure. The castle door opened. Big Alice Eyesore emerged.

As she began the long walk to the center of the field, the cries of kids gathered momentum.

Skinny and Curly watched the consternation, the looks of disgust and horror on the faces of the teachers, and they grinned.

"Big Alice is in the best shape I've ever seen her," said Curly. "She can look pretty scroungy, you know."

"Do you think it's okay, her going in without any armor, Curly?"

"She didn't want any, and she knows best. She's got the three weapons, and that's more than she needs."

Big Alice was enjoying herself. The shocked cries and whispers filtering down from the stands were music to her ears. She slowed her gait and smiled. She was in no hurry to meet her challenger, but she was supremely confident. She wanted attention now because the struggle would be short. She ambled along, basking in the panic she provoked. She even began to show off a bit, opening her mouth to yawn, and when she heard the teachers gasp, she rolled her eyes and dribbled. Two lady kindergarten teachers passed out.

The kids waved their arms and laughed and shouted all sorts of encouragements. Big Alice, who had suffered at the hands of her peers as often as at teachers', loved every minute of it.

Big Alice's parents sat quietly in the crowd, sad and embarrassed. They wore large, wide-brimmed hats and oversized sunglasses, so no one would recognize them.

Around Big Alice's bony frame hung a colorful muumuu pulled in by a wide blue silk sash. Stuck into the sash were an axe, a sword, and a dagger. They were a nuisance to Big Alice, but Skinny had insisted she abide by the rules of the tournament. Now, she pulled them out of her sash and dashed them arrogantly to the ground. She suddenly started to race toward Commodore Putsch, and the crowd gasped. It took all of the

Commodore's strict training to keep him from retreating. But Big Alice was merely teasing; about a yard away from the elm tree, she stopped short and sat down. The crowd started to breathe again when the door to the replica of the Teachers' Cartels Retirement Home and Savings and Loan opened and a dazzling figure stepped out into the full glare of the sunlight.

It was a small, slender person, sheathed entirely in armor. The helmet had hinged sidepieces fastened by leather straps covered with glittering bits of mosaic glass. A small circular disk projected from the back of the helmet and a collar in front, all studded with zircons. A necklet of chain mail fixed by a line of gold rivets went about the collar. From the comb of the helmet waved a colossal purple plume. The breast and back plates and the small, movable sections over the armpits all were delicately chased and engraved. Semi-precious stones glittered in the sunlight, blinding the spectators.

The flamboyant figure moved slowly towards the center of the field. In the right hand was an axe with a blade on one side and a steel barb on the other. The left hand held a shield picturing a fist clasping a rose. The words *Le Chevalier Rococo* encircled the border of the shield.

"Ooh's" and "Ah's" broke a long hush, and all the teachers broke into roars of applause.

Barley turned to Fritzi in the judges' box and whispered, "Who is he?"

"I don't know," whispered back Fritzi. "But don't worry, he hasn't got a chance."

Across the field, Skinny shook his head and cracked his knuckles hard. "What does *Rococo* mean, Curly?" he asked.

"It means overdone."

As the din grew louder, Commodore Putsch took up his gavel and hit the shield which said *Guerre*.

Big Alice stood up. Her nostrils quivered as she glared at her opponent.

Several kids yelled: "The axe! The axe! Go get your axe, Big Alice!"

Big Alice, without taking her eyes off the knight, slowly moved to where she had dropped the axe and picked it up.

The Rococo Knight leisurely approached. When he was several yards away, he stopped.

Big Alice saw the eyes inside the brilliant visor. She squinted and raised her axe.

The knight raised his.

They cast their axes at the same instant. The axes met in midair. There was a terrible *crack!* Big Alice's axe head flew off its handle. The Rococo Knight's axe fell, intact, and lay buried in the grass, handle up.

The knight and Big Alice rushed toward each other.

Big Alice got to the axe first, yanked it up, and faced her assailant.

"Kill him! Kill him!" yelled the kids.

The Rococo Knight took a step back and raised his shield.

Big Alice sprang toward the knight, and the axe struck a terrible blow to the knight's helmet. He reeled back. Big Alice, axe raised, had readied herself for another blow when the knight's helmet fell from his head in two pieces, and dangled from his shoulders.

A loud sigh came from the crowd and binoculars were trained on the knight. A great cry of recognition rose from the stands. The Rococo Knight was Mr. Heather! No doubt about it. The blond hair, the pale face belonged to the Scratchland School art teacher, and a wave of pride rolled like a breaker through the Scratchland teachers.

"Who would have believed it!" cried Miss Jenny Dunphy, who sat with her sister, Miss Bambi, in one of the front rows.

Miss Bambi said nothing. But she looked grim.

The kids were ecstatic. Mr. Heather wouldn't have a chance against Big Alice Eyesore. Yet Skinny sat anxiously on his seat. In the warmth of the sun he sat chilled. Something inside him began chewing, chewing, and his hands shook.

"Hey, Skinny, cheer up!" cried Curly. "Old Mr. Purple Feather is gonna get clobbered!"

The two champions faced each other. They made a peculiarly peaceful tableau in the sunlight.

"Swords!" called out Commodore Putsch.

The stadium echoed: "Swords! Swords!"

Big Alice raced to the fence where she had dropped her sword, retrieved it, and faced her challenger.

The Rococo Knight faced her, sword in hand.

The fight began.

"Where did she ever learn to use a sword, Curly?" asked Skinny.

"She got hold of my King Arthur book and read it over and over. She even made a wooden sword and practiced every day."

Whacking, thrusting, slashing, Big Alice and the art teacher danced about, trading blow for blow. The clang of sword striking sword filled the enclosure. The kids were hollering themselves hoarse, and the teachers screamed.

Curly glanced at Skinny. "Skinny, what's the matter?"

Skinny was pale. He stared into space, mumbling to himself.

"Daggers!" cried the loud voice of Commodore Putsch.

Two kids and two teachers raced out to the field. The adversaries were again frozen, gazing at each other. The squires picked up the swords and dashed away.

"Begin! *A la mort!*"

The Commodore's voice broke their trance, and the two champions rushed at each other, daggers raised.

The spectators gasped and rose to their feet. Big Alice and the Rococo Knight lunged and locked onto each other. They feinted, jabbed, broke apart. Mr. Heather's hoarse breathing could be heard, and the teachers were terrified.

Slash! A long red line appeared on the knight's cheek.

The teachers groaned.

He swayed and fell to his knees. Only his armor saved him from a crushing blow to the chest.

Big Alice was in command. The kids were wild with excitement. The teachers shrieked.

Mr. Heather's dagger flew from his hand and he crumpled. Big Alice, a terrible look on her hairy face, raised her weapon.

Mr. Heather lay on his back, shield over his head, as if waiting for the coup de grace.

Unexpectedly, Big Alice jumped away, howling. Her nose twitched, her arms and legs jerked into a spasmodic dance, and screams tore from her throat. Her lips foamed.

"Watch out, Big Alice! Watch out!" the kids screamed as the Rococo Knight staggered to his feet, dagger in the air. But like a marionette dropped by its master, Big Alice collapsed in a shuddering heap.

The Rococo Knight raised his head to the stands. His face broke into a smile, and he raised his arm in victory. The Teachers threw their lesson plans up into the air, hugged each other, whistled, screeched, and started running down to the field.

"Oh no!" moaned Barley Chops.

Curly said nothing. He turned away so no one would see his tears.

The Kids were stupefied.

As the Rococo Knight made his way to the judges' stand, a cloud passed over the sun and Skinny, pale as chalk, slumped in his seat.

Sterling Guts trained his glasses on Skinny and smiled as the sky blackened with dozens of helicopters.

17

A Visit from Snitch

Within minutes, the helicopters had landed and dozens of officers from the Police Teachers' Academy streamed onto the field to surround and isolate group after group of kids. The officers were aided by hundreds of "foreign observers," teachers from other lands, hard-nosed types recruited by the Foreclosure Institute.

Most kids were in a state of shock and put up little resistance. They were herded into the Savings and Loan and locked in heavily guarded rooms.

Big Alice had been spirited away to the Scratchland Nurse's Office, where all attempts to revive her failed. Though she was breathing, she remained unconscious. A committee of Arts and Humanities Resource teachers were chosen immediately to ready Big Alice as a three-dimensional artifact for a new unit of study, Rampant Kidness: Its Origins and Demise.

Skinny and the other leaders were hustled to a tent in the Kids' encampment by a group of older men dressed in sweat shirts with East Area Janitorial Association sewn on the front. The men were unsmiling and rough. One, the only black man, looked familiar to Skinny.

There was something in his eyes that made Skinny pause and try to remember him. But the moment passed, and Skinny was left with his friends in the tent, plunged into gloom.

Curly peeked out. "We're surrounded," he said and wheeled about, his thumb poised before his face. "Guess it's terminal, expiration. In other words, *finale.*"

Fritzi scowled so angrily that Curly pushed his thumb into his mouth quickly and reddened.

Barley picked up a stick and nervously scratched a hole in the ground. "Guts told me Big Alice is alive but she won't wake up."

"Where is she?" asked Skinny dully.

"They put her in a glass case at the Scratchland library. They're going to study her."

"Teachers are hot on anything under glass," answered Curly, searching his pockets for a stick of gum.

"Exhibits," hissed Fritzi. "Exhibits don't make noise and they stay put. Teachers are fond of exhibits."

Skinny looked up at his friends. "How come they had a glass case so handy for Big Alice?"

Barley frowned. "I reckon they were pretty sure of winning."

Curly stopped sucking and gave Skinny a sharp look. "How could they be so sure?"

"Poor Alice," said Fritzi. "She tried her very best and she was great. Right up to the end." Fritzi's voice faded. The ominous threat of the Status Quo Solidifier haunted her. It was a punishment they had never dreamed would happen to them.

An hour passed. The air felt close, as if a storm threatened. A light rain pattered on the tent.

Little Curly pretended to read a book. Barley was carving a whistle from a stick of bamboo. Skinny sat alone, chewing at his hands. Fritzi was polishing her medals. Frantic scratching near the tent flap startled them. Fritzi lifted the flap, and in leaped Snitch, carrying a scroll between his teeth.

He went over to Skinny and dropped the scroll at his feet. He looked up at each kid, growled, and backed away to the entrance.

Barley raised his hand. "Get outa here, you miserable excuse for a dog!"

Snitch barked and vanished through the tent flap.

Skinny picked up the scroll and unrolled it as Barley, Fritzi, and Curly crowded about him.

"They have Alice. It says . . . we're to accept . . . unconditional surrender . . . and that tomorrow morning . . ." For a moment, Skinny couldn't go on. "We're to . . . submit . . . to the . . . Status Quo Solidifier."

Curly started to laugh, a terrible laugh. Tears ran down his cheeks. He went off to a corner and hid his face in his hands.

"There's nothin' we can do, Skinny, is there?" Barley asked.

"No," replied Skinny, his hands shaking. "Nothing."

18

The End—or the Beginning?

Congratulatory messages poured into Scratchland School. Some were addressed to Dr. Pucker, some to Mr. Foreclosure, and a great many to the Rococo Knight—"The Teachers' Champion." The Scratchland staff was thrilled by greetings from the most distinguished names in education. There was a night letter from Dr. Catalogue of the Buttress School of Business, Impetigo, New Zealand, and a bouquet of roses from Miss Luella Longchamps of Marblehead, Maine, who ran the famous Tigris and Euphrates Piranha Farm for Intractable Children. Mordecai Barf sent a letter. He was dean of Concordia Agricultural Institute and the renowned inventor of Disclosure, a secret TV camera placed in kids' jean pocket rivets. Barf never communicated with anyone except by closed-circuit TV.

Few teachers had gone home. Most remained for the Public Solidification Program which was to take place the next morning, following the Midnight Torchlight Parade and Victory Rally. It would be a historic event, one no Teacher would be likely to forget.

The Kids would forget it immediately. Solidification would be a fast and painless procedure, lasting less than ten seconds. As Dr. Kockamoon put it, "It feels like being hit with a spitball." But the kids would emerge from the S.Q.S. with thinning hair, watery eyes, and wrinkles on their foreheads. The first thing a solidified kid would say was: "What can I do for extra credit?" The leaders would be the last to be solidified, and the honor of pressing the button would be given to the Rococo Knight.

Curly, after hours of silent weeping, had dropped off to sleep, thumb in his mouth. Barley snored vociferously till dawn. Fritzi lay awake and kept doing push-ups.

Skinny could not sleep either. The last moments of the conflict between Big Alice and Mr. Heather came back to him again and again, and each time he groaned. His orange hair curled sticky and damp over his forehead as he paced the tent. Only when the first light streaked the sky did he sit down. His face was chalk-white and his freckles blood-red. He gnawed his fingernails and muttered to himself.

Barley stirred and woke. He placed a large, tanned hand on Skinny's shoulder. His wide gray eyes were warm with a magnetism which few teachers ever saw. "Don't fret so, Skinny. We'll come out of it. I know we will."

Barley looked at Skinny's face and the bony wrists which twitched in his lap. Skinny had heard nothing he said.

A hand with frizzled gray hair on it pushed through the tent flap. One of the men from the East Area Janitorial Association stood in the door. His presence was felt like a shock wave, bringing all the kids to their feet.

The custodian put on a pair of spectacles and read, slowly, from a paper which he held at arm's length. "Bartholomew Chops."

Barley leaped up, grimacing. "I been in six Foreclosure camps, and no Solidifier is going to scare *me!*"

"Anatole Winkler."

"Adios, au revoir, auf wiedersehen, all! Pax vobiscum!" Wearing a tight little smile, Curly wiggled his wet thumb at his friends.

"Fritzi Nissenbaum."

Fritzi touched her medals.

The janitor gazed at Skinny. "You stay. They're saving you for dessert," he added.

The kids turned toward Skinny, holding out their hands. Skinny solemnly shook each one. Barley handed his whittled sticks to Skinny, and then, without a word, the three kids slipped out of the tent after the janitor.

The Status Quo Solidifier stood in the center of the stadium. It was eight feet high, a white box with a door that had a series of lights on it. ("Humph!" sniffed Jenny Dunphy to her sister, Bambi, "Looks like a silly refrigerator!")

The stadium was packed with teachers, all in an exultant mood, waving to one another and bleacher-hopping. Secondary teachers were actually talking to elementary teachers.

The solidification program began with a number of formal speeches by famous educators. Each speaker praised the work of Mr. Foreclosure. Finally, Sterling Guts stood up to speak and was greeted by long applause. Guts's speech was brief. After contributing his share of compliments to Mr. Foreclosure, he introduced the teachers' champion, Mr. Heather, splendidly dressed in a dazzling red silk shirt and matching velour trousers. A three-minute ovation followed, then Mr. Heather was given the honor of unfurling a banner to signal the start of the solidification of the kids.

There was complete silence when the kids were led into the arena. Surrounded by members of the Gym Teachers' Association, the kids were marched in, to line up in rows before the Solidifier. They all had brown paper bags over their heads. A few of the younger kids shook with sobs, but most were silent, heads down and knees trembly. Teachers leaned forward, and hundreds of field glasses were lifted. TV crews were filming, and at each end of the amphitheater, two giant TV monitors on fifty-foot towers came to life.

Dippy O'Toole had been chosen as the first kid to be placed in the Status Quo Solidifier. He was famous for never having been introduced to a comb and brush and for growing corn under his nails. Scores of teacher aides craned their necks as Dippy was pushed into the Solidifier. The door closed, a green light went on, and a loud humming pulsed in the air.

Then silence.

After several seconds, an orange light came on. The S.Q.S. door slowly opened.

There stood a Dippy O'Toole with slicked-back hair and scrubbed face, dressed in slacks and blazer with a monogrammed pocket handkerchief. Scores of binoculars moved from Dippy's face down to his fingernails, and a growing roar of approval filled the arena. The Teachers rose as one and cheered.

Guts whispered to Mr. Foreclosure, hidden behind his tie clasp, "An unmitigated triumph for you, sir!"

A girl named Mary Sindax was next. She came out looking like a costume doll. It went on, kid after kid, hour after hour. All the teachers stayed to watch. It was worth sitting for hours to see a favorite troublemaker go into the Solidifier and come out a Young Person.

As the hours passed, Skinny huddled alone in the tent, waiting his turn. He sat twisted over, his forehead touching the floor. He drifted in and out of consciousness, not hearing the crowd, not feeling anything.

A piece of chalk with no hand holding it, was writing furiously across a blackboard. *Homework overdue: Skinny Malinky. Work sheets late: Skinny Malinky. Makeup test: Skinny Malinky. Tardy offender: Skinny Malinky.* The chalk doubled, tripled, each piece writing now *Skinny's fault, Skinny's fault. The War Between the Pitiful Teachers and the Splendid Kids LOST. Skinny's fault.* The blackboard stretched up to the roof of the tent and was covered by hundreds of sentences. Skinny grabbed an eraser and desperately rubbed at them, but to his horror, the eraser, with a will of its own, wriggled out of his hand and began rubbing *him!* The eraser started at Skinny's fingers. As it traveled back and forth over them, they vanished. Now the eraser was working its way up and down over Skinny's arm, and it disappeared. When the eraser got to his neck, Skinny closed his eyes. Where do all those kids go, he thought wearily, after they get erased? He heard the distant upwelling of thousands of voices. He could feel the whirring wind of the moving eraser over his face, and he cried out.

Skinny opened his eyes. A black hand was lifted from his forehead, where it had lain for a moment.

"Shake it off, Skinny Malinky. Shake it."

Skinny wanted to cling to that voice, but he had fallen too far.

"Good-bye, Ida," he whispered and closed his eyes.

"Why good-bye, Skinny?"

"It's no use. War's over. For good."

"You look at me, Skinny Malinky."

Skinny opened his eyes again.

Ida was wearing a red-and-green bandana. Little beads of perspiration hung on her forehead. A long-handled broom was propped nearby. "They gonna solid'fy you, Skinny."

"I know."

"All kids, I 'spect. They start with the kids here and pick up on the rest they can catch." Ida sat beside him. "You got to move yourself outa here, Skinny. Away from the solid'fy machine."

"No use, Ida. There's nowhere to go."

"You head out straight to tract country. No one's home. Everybody here. I point you the way."

Skinny touched the warm, wrinkled hand. "We lost the tournament, Ida." Then he heaved a sigh and rolled onto his side, with his back to her.

Ida leaned over him. Her powerful hands grasped his

shoulders and she sat him up as if he were a rag doll. His eyes refused to focus on her.

"Listen, Skinny, don't you punish yourself. You got friends you don't even *know*—hear me?"

Skinny nodded.

"Good." She drew a breath. "Not too long ago I was workin' when Miss Jenny and Miss Bambi move in on me and close the door. We talk. They talk. It dark in there and quiet. Are you listenin', Skinny?"

"Yes."

"Miss Jenny say, 'Ida, you got to get to Skinny 'cause he's been tricked. We don't believe in foul play.' That the way she put it."

For the first time, Skinny stirred. He brushed the hair from his eyes and stared. "Tricked?"

"'What you mean, Miss Jenny?' I say. 'Bumpy and I,' she say, 'we talkin' to Mr. Heather and he scared. He been told he going to be the teachers' champ and fight that Big Alice.'"

"Who told him, Ida?"

"Big wheels. The principal, Kratz-man, and that mean-lookin' man in the jump suit—"

"Sterling Guts?"

"Yeah. They pick on Mr. Heather to be champ. He so scared he 'bout melt away, but that Guts man say to Mr. H., 'You *can't* lose. I make *sure* of that.' And he bring Mr. Heather into a locked room—I been in that room, Skinny, dustin' it. It's empty but for a table with a dollhouse on it. Guts say, 'Watch that door.' So Mr. Heather watches and he see the dollhouse door open. And an ant comes out."

"Ant?"

"Yeah, that right, *ant*. Big, red ant. And red ant *talk* to him. Red ant say, 'Mr. Heather, don't you worry. I hide in your sleeve. When you fight Big Alice, I jump on her and *bite*. You win for sure.'"

"A *red ant,* Ida?" Skinny's voice cracked.

"That what Miss Jenny say. Mr. Heather so surprised he nearly faint. He say, '*Who* are you and *how* you talk like that?' This red ant say, 'My name is Fo-closh-er. You hear of me, ain't you?' And Mr. H. say, 'Oh yes sir.'"

A wave of tremors shook Skinny. His fists were clenched at his side.

"Miss Bumpy say this Fo-closh-er important, and so rich he buy whatever he point to. But nobody know he's a little red ant. Now Miss Jenny say, 'Ida, find Skinny Malinky and tell him.' And Miss Bumpy say, 'Teachers need to have *one real kid* around.'

"We all do, Skinny," said Ida. She hugged him. Skinny stood straighter. His red hair blazed.

"Old Jim from Ripley Street School out here, Skinny. He and his buddies see to it you get away."

Skinny looked at Ida. Then he threw his arms around her.

"Go on now! I know you gonna make it."

Skinny lifted the tent flap. The screams of the stadium crowd spurred him to action. He looked back at Ida. Then he began to run.

PART TWO

1

Miss Jenny's Discovery

The teachers at Scratchland were overjoyed to be teaching Young People instead of Kids. They said so, over and over again. However, in quiet moments a few teachers allowed themselves to become nostalgic. Mr. Bullotad, for one. He admitted privately that he missed "the good old days" when there were opportunities to whap a kid over the backside with a wet towel.

Young People did their calisthenics regularly, ran their hearts out on the track, and showered at the drop of a hat. There were no scrawled words in the bathrooms: nary a word. Young People took pride in clean restrooms. There was no end of volunteers to scrub down walls and floors and toilet bowls.

Late one boring afternoon, Miss Jenny and Miss Bambi sat atop two tables in Miss Jenny's classroom.

"Is your door locked, dear?" asked Miss Bambi.

"Oh yes."

Miss Bambi took a long, slim cheroot from her bodice and lit it.

Miss Jenny opened a window and turned on a small fan which sat on a table near the window.

"How was your day, dear?" asked Miss Bambi, exhaling.

"Same as ever. Boring." Miss Jenny fiddled with some papers on her desk, sighing. "Do you remember Beezer Martin?" she asked.

"Of course! Who could forget him! A dreadful kid!" replied Miss Bambi. "The first day he was in my room, the class assignment was to write a short poem on a bird." Miss Bambi bent her head and tittered. "He wrote,

> As I sat under the apple tree,
> A birdie sent his love to me,
> And as I wiped it from my eye,
> I said, Thank goodness, cows can't fly."

Miss Jenny guffawed. Then her face turned sober. "Well," she said, rattling the piece of paper, "you should see him now. He's writing sonnets."

"*Sonnets!*" exclaimed Miss Bambi, flicking an ash skillfully into an inkwell.

"Yes, sonnets. He has written one hundred and fifty sonnets. Twenty-nine sonnet cycles, to be exact."

"Is that a fact?" asked Miss Bambi. "Beezer Martin!"

"It is. The lines all scan, the rhymes are perfect, and the sentiments expressed are those of an octogenarian."

Miss Bambi shook her head. "I wish you hadn't told me." She began to pace about, nervously puffing on her cigar.

"Bumpy, dear?"

"Yes, Jenny?"

"You are spending a lot of time in the library. Are you doing some research?"

"No. It's just . . . that it calms me . . . sitting near Big Alice."

"Aaah yes. I understand."

"Yes. It's quiet there." Miss Bambi stubbed out her cigar and carefully opened a large handkerchief and deposited the butt in its center, which already held four others like it. She dumped into it the contents of the inkwell and, folding the hankie gingerly, she put it back in her blouse.

"I enjoy being with her but I can't tell you why," continued Miss Bambi. "She's quite still but she looks ferociously alive."

"I've felt the same way," replied Miss Jenny. "You know, Bumpy, I've been doing a lot of reading lately on bites."

Miss Bambi looked at her sister quizzically. "Bites?"

Miss Jenny whispered, "Ant bites."

"Have you found anything *significant?*" she asked, whispering back.

"No. Nothing yet." Miss Jenny walked over to a pencil sharpener, undid the top, and emptied it into her hand. Three wrapped pieces of hard candy dropped into her palm. "They come to class now with fresh, sharpened pencils. And they never break the points. Disgusting!" She unwrapped a candy. "Want one? Licorice."

Her sister put out her hand. There was a long silence as they thoughtfully sucked.

"I suspect it was a *sting,*" Miss Jenny said. "Remember that box of strange old books Uncle Willard left us in the cellar? Well, I've been going through them."

"Poor Big Alice," interrupted Miss Bambi. "If only she'd wake up. Did I tell you, Jenny, that I've decided to make Big Alice the subject of my term project in my in-service sculpture class?"

"That won't make you very popular."

"Well, no matter. It's going to be a surprise. And I don't care if I get an A on it or not. I've already made some sketches."

"Let's go home," said Miss Jenny.

The Dunphys lived in an old, ramshackle house in a section of town where no one had air conditioning or garbage disposals. The lots were spacious and filled with trees and shrubs, and the sisters would not have traded their home for the grandest apartment in Bird of

Paradise Homes, where most of their colleagues lived. The fact that the Dunphys preferred their tree-canopied yard, insects and all, to the new high-rise's "wrap-around patios" did not make any sense to the other teachers. The sisters were considered odd.

When they got home, Miss Bambi showed Miss Jenny her sketches.

"They're quite good," responded Miss Jenny.

Miss Bambi beamed and went to work on the sculpture. It was life-size.

She worked on it in the basement every evening. Keeping her company in a huge, overstuffed chair, Miss Jenny riffled the pages of book after book that came from an ancient, cavernous trunk.

"I wonder what has happened to Skinny Malinky," Miss Bambi said one night, apropos of nothing. She laid down her sculpting tools and drank long from a glass of herb tea.

Miss Jenny looked up over her spectacles. "No idea. If he'd been caught, we'd have heard. Bumpy dear, you are a genius!" Miss Jenny stood up and inspected the statue, cocking her head and smacking her lips.

"Do you really like it?"

Jenny walked slowly around the sculpture. "You've caught Big Alice just as she is, asleep and yet *not* asleep! It's the best thing you've ever done!" Miss Jenny went over to her sister and kissed her.

Indeed, Miss Bambi Dunphy's work was remarkably lifelike. The figure lay prone, just as Alice did in the Scratchland library. The eyes were open, mouth curled in shock and surprise, exactly as she had looked when she collapsed at the tournament.

Miss Jenny sighed and went back to her books. A few minutes passed.

Then a shriek tore the silence.

Miss Bambi jumped. "Goodness, Jenny! Whatever is the matter? Are you all right?"

Miss Jenny pressed an open book against her bosom. Her face was flushed, her eyes very bright. "I've found it!" Miss Jenny read softly from her book: " 'This large and ferocious member of the family Formicidae'—meaning *ant*, Bumpy—'this large and ferocious member sometimes displays amazing intelligence. Because of this, a number of curious myths have arisen throughout various epochs of recorded history regarding the so-called mental prowess of this unusual insect. The Babylonians believed that upon every tenth lunar year, during the vernal equinox, the queen conceived an ant possessing human powers.' " Miss Jenny stopped.

"Go on," said Miss Bambi, in a hoarse voice.

" 'The Chaldeans as well as the Sumerians believed also in the supernatural powers of insects, in particular, the red ant.' "

"Red ant," Miss Bambi whispered. "Oh my! What book is that, Jenny?"

"It's called *Odd and Unknown Practices of Dead Civilizations*. But listen, Bumpy, to this: 'The bite of this red ant, unlike the bite of any others of its species, possesses the peculiar faculty of rendering the victim speechless and in a paralytic condition.' " Taking a breath, she continued, " 'The only known antidote to this bite is engraved on an antique tablet that was found in Toltec ruins at the Wilson-Haversham archeological site in Central Mexico, late June, 1823. The hieroglyphics on the tablet report that the leaf, *Sassafras albidum*, steeped in hot liquid, produces a vapor which, if passed over the area of the bite, will cause the victim to regain consciousness. If the leaf is taken internally, the paralysis will dissipate itself.' "

Miss Jenny placed a bookmark between the pages and slowly closed the book. In a very low voice, she said, "Bumpy dear. We shall bring Big Alice to life again." She pointed to the statue. *"And not one person will know!"*

2

Miss Bambi Rings the Bell

At the stroke of midnight, two figures moved through the darkness from the parking lot into Scratchland. Miss Bambi wore a Groucho Marx nose-and-mustache and Miss Jenny was a Frankenstein monster. The monster was wheeling a grocery cart, and on it was balanced a large object swaddled in blankets. Groucho produced a key and opened the door to the Scratchland library.

Pushing the cart ahead of them (the wheels had been well oiled), the two sisters entered the room, then softly closed the door. A flashlight beam cut through the air, coming to rest on the dais where Big Alice lay sleeping.

It took all the Dunphys' strength and much huffing and puffing to lift Big Alice out of the glass case and set her carefully on a table. The sisters sat for several moments, catching their breath and listening for unexpected footfalls. Then they heaved up Miss Bambi's wax statue and placed it in Alice's case. It fit exactly.

"It looks lovely, just like her. The real test will come tomorrow," whispered the monster to Groucho.

Then Big Alice was lifted onto the cart and covered

with blankets, arranged so there was air for her to breathe.

As silently as they had come, the Dunphys exited from the building and wheeled the cart to their Hudson, which was parked behind the library. Transferring Big Alice into the backseat was awkward, but it was finally done, and Groucho drove the auto to the old frame house on Dvořák Street without incident.

The sisters rolled Big Alice into their living room but soon became so jittery they decided Big Alice had to be placed in the basement. Miss Jenny conceived the idea of sliding the hyena girl down the laundry chute, thus saving them the effort of carrying her down a steep flight of stairs.

At last Big Alice lay on a warped Ping-Pong table in a corner of their cellar. Only then did the Dunphys relax, throwing themselves into faded deck chairs, groaning and grunting.

"We've done it!" cried Miss Bambi, and she lit up one of her favorite cigars. "I wasn't sure we could."

"So far, so good," replied Miss Jenny, kicking off her shoes and wiggling her toes. "But the hardest work is ahead. Tomorrow night is Phase Two."

The next morning, Miss Jenny entered the library during her three-minute rest-room break on the pretense that she needed the new filmstrip *Syllabication and Hypnosis*. There were already two other teachers looking for the same strip, because Mr. Snockadocka had narrated it. As Miss Jenny stood in line at the Outgoing Media desk, she stole a look at the dais which dominated the Extinct Kids exhibit. If she had not helped substitute the waxen image herself, she would not have believed that Big Alice Eyesore was now in her cellar. The statue was a perfect replica.

Clutching COPY 3 of the filmstrip, Miss Jenny turned and walked slowly past the dais. She choked and nearly dropped the filmstrip. There, on Big Alice's chest, she saw a square of licorice candy. It must have dropped from her pocket the night before. She stumbled and would have fallen if her sister, Miss Bambi, had not unexpectedly appeared. One look at Miss Jenny and Miss Bambi knew something was wrong. She advanced towards the exhibit, then froze. For a moment, she was as still as the statue.

The voice of the circulation librarian, Miss Haverstock, broke in. "Are you feeling all right, Miss Dunphy?"

Miss Bambi leaped toward the librarian's desk. "No!" she cried. "It's my room! Yes! My *room!*"

"Your room?" Miss Haverstock echoed.

"Yes! My room is on fire!" And, running over to a corner, Miss Bambi yanked the small axe that hung on the wall and smashed the window of the emergency fire bell. Before anyone could move or say a word, Miss Bambi had pulled the chain and the fire bell began yammering a frightful staccato.

Miss Haverstock rushed to the door and out, and as she vanished, Miss Bambi and Miss Jenny ran to the dais, lifted the glass case cover, and drew out the sweet. Miss Bambi dropped it into her pocket.

A stream of teachers and Young People could be seen through the window, gathering in neat lines against the fence.

Miss Jenny laughed so hard she slowly sank to the floor. "Oh, Bumpy . . . you rang . . . a . . . false alarm! *Just like a kid!*"

Later, Miss Bambi made an absolute mess of trying to explain why she had pulled the emergency bell. But Dr. Pucker actually seemed pleased.

"We haven't had a fire drill since the Kids were changed into Young People," he declared to his secretary. "It gave us a chance to evaluate their reaction time."

3

Sassafras Albidum

Miss Bambi felt that in light of Big Alice's reputation, it might be wise to truss her up before *Phase Two* began. Miss Jenny disagreed. If they were to win Big Alice's trust and respect, they should leave her free.

"We've got to show Big Alice that we are her true friends."

"Yes, but remember what happened to Mrs. Jerome," declared Miss Bambi, skeptically shaking her head.

"Well. We are *not* Mrs. Jerome," answered Miss Jenny. Her voice dropped. "If anyone can find Skinny, Big Alice can." She sighed. "And if anyone needs a friend right now, it's poor Skinny."

"I just know he's alive, somewhere," said Miss Bambi. "I feel it in my bones."

They could smell the sassafras steeping upstairs in the kitchen. It came from the large sassafras tree growing in their own backyard. Their neighbors, who called the yard the "Dumpy Jungle," weren't averse to borrowing a pinch of dill or thyme or sassafras occasionally.

"It's ready," said Miss Jenny. She flew up the basement stairs and returned carrying the pot carefully.

Miss Bambi rose and dropped her knitting in the chair.

"It's been steeping now for fifteen minutes," said Miss Jenny. She put the pot down and drew up a chair beside the floor just below Big Alice's head. "Now!" she cried, whipping the lid off the pot. A cloud of aromatic steam escaped, enveloping Big Alice. Miss Bambi waved a large palmetto leaf over the pot.

"Again, Bumpy! Keep it up! She's coming to! She's come to, Bumpy!"

Big Alice's eyes had changed.

The sisters stepped back.

Big Alice's eyes were definitely not friendly. Miss Bambi was alarmed, but Miss Jenny was not.

"Big Alice? Big Alice, can you hear me?" Miss Jenny spoke in her softest and firmest voice. "Don't be afraid. We'll not harm you."

"We want to be your friends," added Miss Bambi, in a quavering voice.

"We *are* your friends," declared Miss Jenny. "We have brought you back to life."

Big Alice did not stir, but there was something in her eyes that would have made any ordinary teacher flinch. But then, Jenny Dunphy was not an ordinary teacher.

"Eat this. It will help you." Miss Jenny held out a bowl of chopped sassafras leaves, still steaming. "Open your mouth," said Miss Jenny, a spoon in her hand.

"She can't yet, Jenny dear," exclaimed Miss Bambi.

"How stupid of me!" muttered Miss Jenny. She took a leaf and forced it between Big Alice's lips.

"Put in another," whispered Miss Bambi.

The leaves had a magical effect. Big Alice moved her lips.

"Swallow! Swallow!" commanded Miss Jenny.

Big Alice swallowed. And then it came. A snarl. What a pitifully weak snarl it was! The sisters looked at each other and smiled.

"You're doing fine, Big Alice. Real fine, isn't she, Bumpy dear?"

Big Alice moved her head, and Miss Jenny held a heaping spoonful of sassafras up to Big Alice's mouth. Slowly, the mouth opened and took the leaves. The jaws moved up and down vigorously.

Big Alice gradually lifted her head and whimpered. Her body shook.

Miss Bambi brought over a quilt, and together the sisters eased Big Alice down again and covered her.

"Keep chewing. It'll help you. Don't worry, we're all alone here."

Big Alice began grinding her teeth, and a frown wrinkled her forehead.

Miss Bambi shuddered.

"You remember now . . . we are your friends," whispered Miss Jenny.

Big Alice sat up. Tossing away the quilt, she got off the table and, ignoring the Dunphys, began moving about the basement, cautiously sniffing and snorting in all its corners. When she had satisfied her curiosity, she sat on her haunches in the center of the floor. Then she raised her head and gave out a first-class, magnificent hyena laugh.

Miss Bambi clutched her sister's hand in panic and delight.

4

Big Alice's Decision

Miss Jenny brought three good-sized raw steaks down to the basement. She unwrapped them and set them on the floor.

Big Alice gobbled them up in about two minutes.

"A good appetite is always encouraging," murmured Miss Bambi, nervously, from a corner.

Big Alice finished eating and sat on the floor, facing the Dunphys. "I don't trust you," she said in a hoarse voice.

"You can leave at any time," said Miss Jenny, "but you should know that it would be highly dangerous. My sister and I are willing to help you if you want to stay here a bit and plan. However, it is up to you. Come, Bumpy dear." Miss Jenny beckoned to her sister, who followed her up the stairs. On the top step, Miss Jenny turned to Big Alice. "If you need anything, come upstairs. We will be in the sitting room having our tea."

Big Alice made another tour of the basement, snuffling and grunting. She suspected a trick. And yet why had the Dunphys bothered to bring her back to life?

Suddenly, a familiar odor made her nose twitch. The odor, mixed with the smell of earth, excited her. She stared at the floor. It was a concrete floor, old and in need of repair. Placing her nose to the floor, she followed the scent until she tracked it to three long cracks in the concrete in the furnace room. She closed her eyes. The odor bristled with portent. She read a silent signal, an important message which she was unable to decipher. She traced the cracks with her hairy fingers and noticed that the cracks joined and seemed to form a rough triangle. She looked around, and saw some tools hanging on a wall: a hammer, a screwdriver, pliers, a chisel. She took the chisel and forced it into a crack. Pushing as hard as she could, she leaned on the chisel. The block moved, gave a quarter of an inch. She strained, but she needed more strength than she had to move the concrete block. After more useless prying, she gave up and placed the chisel back on the wall. Then she climbed the stairs to the Dunphys' living room.

The sisters were pouring tea. They had been conversing in low voices but were still when Big Alice appeared.

Big Alice walked on all fours to the center of the room and then stood up on her hind legs. Folding her arms—as she must have remembered seeing teachers do—she said: "Skinny. I want to see Skinny."

Miss Bambi and Miss Jenny peered at one another, concerned and careful. After a pause, Miss Jenny stood up.

"Skinny is gone, Big Alice," she said gently. "He escaped. All the other kids have been . . . solidified."

Big Alice looked confused. "I raised my dagger. . . . I raised my dagger . . ." she mumbled, looking up at Miss Jenny. "What happened?" She took a step forward. "You better tell me."

Miss Jenny's heart began skittering about in her chest, but she stood her ground. "I'll be glad to, Big Alice." She cleared her throat. "At the crucial point when you were about to vanquish your adversary, the Rococo Knight—"

"Mr. Heather, the art teacher," interjected Miss Bambi.

"Yes, that's right, Mr. Heather, the art teacher. At the crucial point, Mr. Foreclosure, hidden inside Mr. Heather's sleeve, jumped on you and bit you. His bite, though not fatal, produced immediate paralysis."

Seeing the puzzled look on Big Alice's face, Miss Bambi explained softly: "Mr. Foreclosure is a vicious, red ant. That is, physically he is a red ant. Mentally, he is human."

"Mr. Heather told us about him before the tournament. He was frightened, and it's clear he was telling the truth. In case you have not heard of him, Big Alice, Mr. Foreclosure is very rich, powerful, and quite ruthless. Among other things, he is chairman of Scratchland's Board of Education. Of course, it's a secret that he's a red ant, and Sterling Guts does his dirty work."

Big Alice turned from one sister to the other. "You mean . . . I really *lost* the tournament?"

"Yes, dear," replied Miss Jenny, her hands straying nervously to her hair. "You lost. And the kids were put into the Status Quo Solidifier. Except for Skinny, there are no more kids. They are all Young People now."

Big Alice shook her head wildly. She gnashed her teeth with a terrible grinding noise. "What happened to Skinny?" she said at last.

"He was going to be solidified, but in the nick of time Skinny escaped. With a bit of help."

"Yes," whispered Miss Bambi, "and that is why we must be so careful. The gym teachers are supposed to be out in force searching for him. Mr. Foreclosure's agents are everywhere."

"Where—did—he—go?"

Miss Jenny raised her hands. "We don't know, but he's still free. We certainly would have heard if he'd been captured."

"I want something to eat," Big Alice said rudely and slunk down the cellar stairs.

134

Miss Jenny carried down two halibut steaks, half a chicken, and several soup bones. To these Miss Bambi added two pounds of raw liver and a freshly baked loaf of banana bread. Big Alice signaled the sisters away with a surly twist of her lips and devoured everything that had been set before her.

After all the food, she sat in a torpor but her mind raced. The name of Mr. Foreclosure rang a bell deep inside and made her restless. Somewhere in the Lake Cachuma Wildlife Preserve was the summer home of Mr. Foreclosure. He leased thousands of acres from the Forest Service for lumbering and mining. Once, Big Alice had seen the walled compound of the summer home and had been unsettled by it. Ever since, she had avoided it.

But now, in the dark of the cellar, she grew homesick for the preserve and for her friends, the great horned owl named Hooter and the hyena she called Rudy.

With a whine, she dismissed these thoughts and loped over to the concrete block. Poking about, she discovered an iron pole that had once belonged to a swing set. With hammer and chisel, she attacked the triangular stone until she had loosened it at various points. When she inserted one end of the iron pole under a corner and pushed down with all her strength, the slab lifted at the opposite corner and fell over, uncovering a large hole.

Big Alice leaned over it to look down. The unmistakable odor of *kid* wafted out! Big Alice sniffed, her nostrils wide. She peered down again. There was nothing to see. She dropped a pebble into the hole and counted to three. She heard it land.

She needed a flashlight. In an old chest of drawers near the stairs she found one, and she flashed it down the hole. The bottom appeared to be dry and firmly packed, so Big Alice scrambled down the hole. The flashlight then disclosed what she had been unable to see from the surface—the entrance to a tunnel. The

135

tunnel was roomy and airy and very dry. Big Alice walked into it slowly.

It must have taken her ten minutes to reach a wide space where the tunnel divided into two. She played the light back and forth from one tunnel to the other. The smell that came from the tunnel on the right was rank, but there was no doubt that intermingled with the odor of sewer was the smell of—*kid!*

Big Alice inhaled deeply. She moved her light as far down the passage as she could, and noticed something on the wall of the right-side tunnel. She moved closer. Words! Printed clumsily in red paint on the damp, concrete wall, they read:

TO LAKE CACHUMA

5

Hooter

Hooter was outstanding in a family of birds well known for intelligence. But as a baby, Hooter had fallen out of his nest in the wildest section of the Lake Cachuma Wildlife Preserve. Big Alice had found and cared for him. He grew to be very handsome, with enormous, fiery, yellow red eyes, two large, feathered ear tufts, and striking black-and-brown plumage. He was a magnificent great horned owl, a giant among his species, with powerful talons and beak and a six-foot wingspan. He could converse with Big Alice and her cousin, Rudy, in a language half sound, half silence. He could tell Big Alice about the things he saw in his flights over the preserve. Though human behavior often puzzled him, the bird listened to Big Alice and attempted to understand those things which interested her. The two became inseparable.

When Big Alice left for Scratchland, Hooter brooded for days. When she did not return, Hooter decided to leave the preserve and look for her.

Unlike an ordinary owl, Hooter could see well even in daytime. Flying east, he passed one deserted school after another. There was much traffic on the roads, innumerable cars and buses. The buses had banners attached to their sides. One banner read: Teachers Über Alles. Hooter flew on for most of the day and stopped only at dusk, to rest near a reservoir. Then, after dining on a jackrabbit and several grasshoppers, he spread his wings and resumed his flight. He missed the security of Lake Cachuma, but a sense of urgency stronger than fear drew him closer to Scratchland.

All at once, the smell of *kid* spiraled up to the bird. It gave him pleasure. Far below, there were thousands of tents and bicycles. Hooter's spirits soared as he dropped downwards, talons outspread. The camp was empty. Hooter perched atop the center pole of one of the tents and blinked his eyes.

There! Now he caught it!—the scent of Big Alice! He rose, and as he gained height he saw below him hundreds of humans scuttling about like sowbugs. Long lines of humans flowed from a huge, roofless structure. Again the odor of Big Alice reached Hooter, stronger now, and the bird wheeled anxiously over the stadium, looking for her.

Hooter flew back and forth over Scratchland until dusk. Then he hunted for his dinner in the deserted amphitheater. There were rats about, and Hooter ate his fill. He sat on a bare flagpole and ruffled his feathers irritably. Then he hooted. There was nothing here. The scent of Big Alice had faded. He must return to Lake Cachuma.

As the owl flew west, he looked in vain for kids. At many schools Hooter saw crowds of adults racing back and forth between buildings, carrying things to burning piles. One huge pile in a school yard consisted of jump ropes, beanbags, deflated balls, and baseball bats. Hooter passed over one school where teams of people were breaking up jungle gyms and other play equipment. At another, a group of women, all wearing black jerseys printed with the words Kindergarten Teachers for Cleaner Floors, were splitting sandboxes with picks and axes and carting off the sand in wheelbarrows.

Hooter gave up looking for kids. He headed for

home, and as night fell, Lake Cachuma shimmered beneath him.

Hooter made his way to one of Big Alice's old haunts in the densest part of the Lake Cachuma Wildlife Preserve. There, on a branch of his favorite live oak, he settled.

Beneath the tree lay an animal the size of a wolf. Its fur was grayish-brown, and it bore stripes of a darker shade along its sides. Its ears were large and pointed. A mane, stiff as wire, extended along the back to the tail. The tail was short and bushy and lay flat. This was Rudy, the hyena, companion of Big Alice Eyesore and an old friend of Hooter's.

Rudy gave attention to an itch in his paw.

Hooter blinked.

No one is sure what's happened to the kids. They are nowhere, said Rudy. He crouched, placed his nose between his paws, and snuffled. The owl cocked his head.

Only the kid called Skin-nee Ma-lin-kee has escaped. The birds say he's running.

Hooter seemed to grow bigger. His pinions quivered, sending some leaves down on the hyena.

Hooter was aloft.

Who was Skin-nee Ma-lin-kee? Was he a friend—a friend of Big Alice's?

Hooter would go back and look again.

6

Flight

Skinny was running.

He was in tract country. *Pleasure Dome Homes. Blacktop driveways, split-level, tri-level lots, closets galore, fenced rear yard, lifetime aluminum with a no-life warranty. SEE AND APPRECIATE more living for pennies. HOME SWEET HOME PLEASURE DOME.*

Sprinting by the tiny new trees, artificial ivy, concrete lawns, miniature fences, tricycles, plastic balls, and dolls, through the oily carports. Skinny was running.

And in every empty living room, a color TV alive with a rerun of the tourney. Skinny saw Big Alice pitch forward and fall again and again, in window after window. He felt sick from the TVs' blaring, from the News of the Century, the War Between the Teachers and the Kids, the Triumph of the Teachers, the Fall of Big Alice Eyesore, over and over and over. . . .

Skinny was running. But he didn't know where. Drop beneath a car. Cock an ear.

Come to Mt. Olympus! Drywall construction! Full cathedral ceilings!

Panting for breath, Skinny squatted in the shadow of the billboard.

The model homes sat sleeping. A printed card was looped around the doorknob of model number one (Mediterranean Ranch style). It read: Closed for the Tourney—Be Back Later, and in smaller handwriting: *Give it to 'em, Teachers!*

Skinny pressed his forehead down on his knees, pushing on his brain. Then he was running again, lost in the ocean of Too Good To Pass Up.

Bliss Haven Ahead. Genuine Woodburning Fireplaces!

Skinny was gasping now, taking gulps of air and exhaling noisily. He trembled from head to foot.

The slam of a car door, and voices; Skinny was in a hawthorn bush, with spikes slashing at him.

"Almost ready, Tom?"

"Yep. Just one more load."

Laughter and footsteps.

Skinny dashed to a wall, huddled down, then craned his neck and peered over.

At the end of a cul-de-sac a moving van was parked. The back doors of the van were propped open and a ramp led down to the street. Inside the large truck were heaped old blankets and tarps, some huge crates, and a dolly. On a new sidewalk near the ramp was a rack filled with fur coats. Voices. Skinny ducked down. He placed his hand on his sweaty chest and felt his heart. It would explode like a firecracker and . . .

A door slammed. The motor started.

Then Skinny heard a bark. His chin wobbled, his lips trembled. The tiny fret of a bark belonged to a Pekinese—Snitch!

Skinny straightened up. Again he heard Snitch's bark. It was close. Snitch had scented him!

With his last ounce of strength, Skinny scrambled over the wall and dashed to the van. Once inside, he burrowed beneath a pile of old, ragged blankets beside a packing crate and lay stiff and still. The barking ceased. *Slam-bang!* The two doors to the van shut tight and a wooden bar dropped across them. Skinny heard the cab door shut as a second man settled himself on the seat.

"Let's go, Tom!"

The truck began to move. Skinny swallowed, then crept out from the blankets. Through a crack between the doors he could see a sign on the road that read: Elysium Hills Estates, 75 miles. Then he spotted old Mrs. Solemnsides on a bicycle, half a block away and moving fast. Racing alongside her was Snitch. Skinny shrank back, feeling like an elevator with its cables cut.

7

At Skinny's Heels

No sooner had the moving van turned the corner than old Mrs. Solemnsides hopped down from her bicycle and whistled to Snitch. He sprang into her arms, and she switched on the radio transmitter on Snitch's collar.

"Solemnsides and Snitch here. Over."

"Come in, Solemnsides and Snitch," spoke a voice from the transmitter.

"I'm at Bliss Haven, number 464, and I need reinforcements. Trail very warm. Malinky kid can't be far!"

"Congratulations, Solemnsides and Snitch!" replied the voice. "Stay where you are. I shall contact Tests and Measurements immediately. Await further instructions. Roger."

"Good, good!" murmured old Mrs. Solemnsides. Dropping Snitch, she opened her purse and she took out a tiny, beveled mirror. She looked at herself and was pleased. She was wearing the same bicycle dress she had worn fifty-five years before when she had gone cycling in the Vienna woods with an Austrian cavalry officer. The dress, though it smelled of camphor and rosewood, was as good as new. She sat down on the curb, fussing with the tortoiseshell combs holding her bun in place. Snitch sat beside her, his purple tongue lolling out.

"Did you hear that, pet?" chirped the old lady, patting the dog. "Tests and Measurements. It won't be long now!"

Tests and Measurements, Dear Reader, was the name that referred to four very special teachers: Dr. Allen Carsik, Dr. Lena Kanker, Dr. No Kan Doo, and Dr. Norman Norms. These four teachers were responsible for creating the tests given to all kids between the ages of four and a half and seventeen. "By his test score shall ye know him" was their dictum. They had also worked on the Status Quo Solidifier.

These four doctors had been busily subjecting a photo of Skinny Malinky to a battery of tests in their laboratory at Sandcastle University. When the phone rang summoning them to join old Mrs. Solemnsides at the housing tract, they had just completed a personality assessment of Skinny. It gave an in-depth picture of his home environment, including such data as average monthly totals of tub baths taken and comic books read.

Accompanied by none other than Dr. Kuzma Kockamoon, the inventor of the S.Q.S., their truck arrived within the hour at 464 Bliss Haven, with a load of fancy electronic equipment.

"We've lost the scent," said Mrs. Solemnsides grumpily. "My Snitch just keeps growling and running in circles!"

The five doctors prowled about.

Dr. Kockamoon was on all fours at the curb, examining a large oil stain. "According to the Kuder-Richardson formulas," he said, "I can estimate safely within the normal unit distribution curve that a truck has recently parked here."

Dr. Lena Kanker opened her purse and perused her Reliability Tables. Then, snapping the purse shut, she exclaimed, "Based on Empirical Criterion Keying, and

144

employing the Frumkin Forced-Choice technique, I have no doubt that *Skinny Malinky is on that truck.*"

Each doctor shook Dr. Kanker's hand.

Old Mrs. Solemnsides stood, weight back on her heels, arms akimbo. "Well, what shall we *do?* Gracious, we can't just stand here shaking hands all afternoon!"

Dr. Norms turned to the old lady with a disapproving stare. "He is as good as caught, Mrs. Saluset. Just tell us which way the truck went."

"Towards Elysium Hills Estates," cried old Mrs. Solemnsides. "And my name is Solemnsides."

"We've got him then," chortled Dr. Carsik. "There isn't a thing I don't know about Elysium Hills Estates! I live there."

They all scrambled into the truck. Mrs. Solemnsides, with Snitch in her arms, was sitting on Dr. Kockamoon's lap.

As Dr. Carsik started the engine, he said, "I've recently made a Factor Analysis of Assessment on this make of truck. Highly probable that it will take us directly to where we are going!"

The other Testers nodded soberly, and the truck lurched forward at a good, smart speed.

8

Encounter at Elysium Hills

Skinny was cold. The truck was air-conditioned. He could make out a row of fur coats hanging from a rack above him. Skinny pulled down one of the coats and wrapped himself in it. It was a comfort to Skinny until he noticed that the collar was trimmed with two paws and a small head . . . a mink or a fox. Skinny, in disgust, tossed it away and pulled down a second coat. It was styled the same as the first. Skinny murmured to the two glass eyes that peered at him from under his neck, "You poor dead animal. I'm sorry." The neck-piece somehow reminded him of Big Alice Eyesore, and he shivered. He lay back, pulled another coat over him, and closed his eyes, trying to think of something pleasant.

Skinny was awakened by a cry. It came from his own lips. Fortunately, it was muffled by the noise of the van's braking. The truck stopped. Paralyzed, Skinny heard the cab doors open and shut, the sound of men's voices. There were no steps toward the rear of the van. Skinny crawled to the door and squinted through the crack.

The truck was parked near an enormous billboard: WELCOME TO ELYSIUM HILLS ESTATES!

"How many trucks are there?" called a new voice.

"About a dozen," said one of the drivers.

"Well, just follow this street down to the bay," continued the new voice. "You can't miss it."

The men reentered the truck, and it moved on.

Skinny knew he would have to make a dash for it. Teeth chattering, he leaned his shoulder against the rear doors and felt them give a little. The wooden bar laid across the doors was apparently no thicker than a broomstick. Skinny pushed again. This time the wood almost cracked. A feeling which Skinny had thought dead sparked up in him— Hope. Biting his lip, he backed as far as he could into the van, cleared away the furs, and readied himself for a lunge at the doors. The radio was playing in the cab. There was a good chance they wouldn't hear a thing.

Just as Skinny was aiming a shoulder at the doors, the truck came to a sudden halt, knocking him to the floor.

"Hey, Tom! Long time no see!"

"Where are you headed for?"

"The bay. Deliverin' furs. You been here long?"

"No. Just dropped off a load o' desks at Lake Cachuma." Skinny gasped and held his breath. "Worst roads I ever saw! And I never saw so many cops! Had to have a special pass."

"How come?"

"Who knows? Hey, I'll buy you a cup of coffee."

The men got out of the truck. After a minute of friendly joshing, the voices and footsteps faded away. Skinny, heart pounding, looked out through the crack between the doors. A long line of trucks were parked behind his, all empty. Skinny rushed the doors, the stick broke, and one of the doors swung partially open.

A small dog barked, a sickeningly familiar bark. Skinny dived back into the van, pulling the door shut and drawing the fur coats over him.

The Testers, who had driven at breakneck speed, were grouped about a fireplug several yards away from

Skinny. At the curb was their van, where old Mrs. Solemnsides sat holding Snitch on her lap. He was barking and struggling to get out of the van.

The Testers were looking wise, waiting for something to happen. Snitch wriggled himself free, jumped out of the truck, and yapped furiously at the Testers, as if he were trying to get their attention.

"Watch my Snitch!" screamed old Mrs. Solemnsides. She wanted more than anything in the world for Snitch to find Skinny first. What a coup that would be!

Snitch began running from one truck to another, barking and sniffing.

"Hey, what's the mutt doing? Smells a cat, eh?" said one driver.

Skinny crouched in the van beneath the furs, clenching a small iron bar in his hand. He heard the dog whining and sniffing at the rear doors, and he raised the bar. But Snitch ran off to the next truck. The furs smelled stronger than Skinny did.

The truck drivers were laughing at Snitch. The five Testers looked at one another with smug expressions. Old Mrs. Solemnsides seethed with disappointment as Snitch crawled back into the truck with her, panting and whining.

"Your canine," said Dr. Kockamoon to the old woman, "is of no use except as filler in the better brands of cat food." He smiled over the shoulders of his colleagues at the truck drivers, who burst into a round of spontaneous applause while Skinny sneaked from the rear of the van.

Dodging from one truck to another, he worked his way to the last truck. He crawled beneath it to think out his plan of action.

The drivers were drinking their coffee. Mrs. Solemnsides held tightly to her pet.

In the other direction Skinny could see sunlight glittering on water. There were a dock, canoes, sailboats, motorboats. Head down, arms low to the ground like a chimpanzee, Skinny hurtled out from under the truck towards the dock.

At that moment, Snitch went wild. He nipped his mistress on the shoulder and leaped from her arms. He smelled Skinny, and away he went like a shot!

"It's Skinny Malinky! My Precious has found him!" screamed the old lady. Lifting the skirt of her bicycle dress, she raced after the dog as fast as her old legs could take her. The Testers, jaws open, stared at one another, but the truck driver reacted. *"Kid?"* one of them cried, and in a trice he had caught up with old Mrs. Solemnsides. A truck driver on either side of her lifted her off her feet and carried her along. Though her feet never touched the ground, they kept moving! The five doctors grabbed their briefcases and followed. The chase was on!

Skinny sped like a bullet. The truck drivers were far behind, and Skinny felt euphoric. He could see Lake Cachuma before him, boats bobbing up and down at their slips like toys in a tub. At the first slip lay a trim red-and-white motorboat.

Skinny drew a great breath and looked back at the crowd chasing him. Their yells were faint but distinct: "Give up now or you'll be sorry!" "We'll get ya, kid!" Skinny jumped into the boat.

He had never handled a motorboat. He looked for a wire or rope to pull. Nothing! The pursuers were getting closer, with Snitch about three yards in the lead. Desperately, Skinny pushed and pulled levers and buttons. The engine caught! And raced! A cry of joy escaped Skinny as he turned and yanked a rope from the bow and tossed it free. Skinny found another button and pushed. The boat shot forward. The barking faded as Skinny zoomed out into the bay.

Another boat pulled away from the dock behind him. They were after him! Skinny stared frantically toward the opposite shore. He had to make it before the other boat. Glancing back again, he could make out two boats behind him. They were gaining. At the wheel of the lead boat was none other than Snitch. (Unconventional Techniques of Kid-Pursuit had been the title of Snitch's graduate course at J. Edgar Prime Mover Obedience School.) It took all the little dog's strength to maneuver the wheel, but he managed admirably. As for old Mrs. Solemnsides, she was not in the speedboat with her beloved pet, but rather behind it, attached by a towline, skimming along on water skis! Behind Mrs. Solemnsides was the second boat, loaded with the five famous Testers and three truck drivers.

"I've been thinking, Lena!" shouted Dr. Carsik to Dr. Kanker above the din of the motor. "We must revise our statistical criteria at once! That canine is promising!"

"That's a smart pooch!" yelled one of the truck drivers.

"That old dame ain't so bad!" yelled another in unabashed approbation of old Mrs. Solemnsides.

She was having the time of her life! She had always excelled in sports. Skimming along the choppy waters of the bay, shouting commands to Snitch, she was in her element. The margin between Skinny's boat and hers kept narrowing. It was only a matter of minutes before she would overtake Skinny.

Skinny pushed against the wheel, as if by pushing he might make the boat go faster. The speedometer needle was as high as it could go, and still he could not shake the Pekinese. Snitch was now only a dozen yards astern. Skinny groaned, and at the same instant, an idea popped into his brain. He turned the steering wheel sharply. The boat spun about, and for a moment lay at right angles to the water, almost capsizing. Then it righted itself and, gunning the motor, Skinny pointed his boat straight for Mrs. Solemnsides!

The old woman screamed. Snitch struggled with the wheel, frantically turning to the side.

Roaring down on poor Mrs. Solemnsides, Skinny missed her by two inches! Shrieking, she let go of the towline and fell. The wake of Skinny's boat swamped the Testers' boat and it took in water. Its engine sputtered, then failed.

Skinny waved merrily and buzzed off toward shore.

Snitch was divided between loyalty to his mistress and duty to the chase, but Larger Issues had been core curriculum for him at J. Edgar. Snitch started up his motor again and barked a series of short, encouraging yelps to his owner, who was treading water. Then, pulling out the throttle, he zoomed off. The Larger Issue had won out.

Mrs. Solemnsides was soon picked up by the second motorboat, which had gotten its engine going. But Skinny had gained valuable time.

It began to rain and the wind was working furiously on the water. Skinny reached the far shore. He rammed the boat unceremoniously into a slip and jumped out. Ahead lay a stretch of woods, and Skinny yelled with joy.

To his surprise and horror, two men stepped out from the trees. They wore hunters' caps and had rifles in their hands. Skinny began running down the beach. The men, hallooing after him, took up pursuit.

"It's a *kid!*" one cried.

"Hey, stop, you kid! Or I'll shoot!"

Skinny veered and headed for the trees. Another hunter emerged from the point Skinny was aiming for, throwing Skinny into a panic. Stumbling now, and wheezing great breaths, Skinny faltered, fell, rose again. What direction should he go? Skinny's head swiveled back and forth. He'd take a step in one direction, jerk about, then take a step in another. The cries of the hunters rang in his ears, joined with the barking of the despicable dog, who by now had landed and was racing down the beach.

Skinny slumped and fell. This time he did not rise.

The hunters, Snitch, old Mrs. Solemnsides, holding up the skirt of her wet dress, the Testers, the truck drivers, all were now converging on Skinny. Not one of them saw the dark flying shape in the sky above them, growing larger and larger, plummeting downwards at miraculous speed.

A tremendous bird—some said it was an eagle, some said it was an extinct condor—materialized over Skinny. In a movement so fast that one hunter later said it reminded him of a bolt of lightning, the bird dug its claws into the kid's belt and lifted him into the air.

The hunters stood stock-still. The bird was disappearing when old Mrs. Solemnsides screamed, *"Don't let him get away!"*

The hunters looked at one another, uncertain.

"Shoot him down! Shoot him down!"

The hunters raised their rifles.

"Just a moment, gentlemen," enjoined Dr. Carsik, walking up to the hunters. "The anticipated effects of speed on indices of—"

"Oh hush up!" screamed old Mrs. Solemnsides, completely losing control of herself and shoving the world-famous psychometrist stumbling into his colleagues. The old woman clawed a rifle from a hunter's hands and aimed it at the heavens. She fired.

By now, Hooter (for it was he) was safely out of range. Absolutely beside herself with rage, Mrs. Solemnsides brought the barrel down and fired again. Luckily, she missed Dr. Carsik, but she did considerable damage to his briefcase. The truck drivers firmly took possession of the rifle, and the stricken old woman tottered and fell, weeping. Dr. Carsik fingered his bullet-riddled briefcase dazedly. His face was green.

Snitch opened his purple-black lips and howled.

9

Skinny Finds
a New Friend

Skinny was exhausted from the chase. He hadn't eaten since before the tournament. When Hooter clutched him in his large black talons, lifting him skyward, all that registered in Skinny's mind was the presence of a dark, feathered blanket. He lost consciousness.

It was just as well that Skinny fainted, for Hooter flew at a vast height. If Skinny had opened his eyes and looked down, he would have been terrified. Hooter sensed that what he carried would be an attractive target, and he made sure he was out of even the most far-reaching rifle's range.

Skinny was deadweight, and the distance between the lakeshore and the preserve was long. Hooter's strength was taxed to its limits, but he had the image of Big Alice in his heart and knew he had found a precious link to his friend. He would not relinquish it.

Skinny regained consciousness in a dense thicket. He lay in a dip in the ground where moss and humus were deep.

Skinny lifted his head. It hurt. His thoughts were

confused. The last he remembered was a man striding towards him with a rifle.

But this was not the lakeshore. Where was he? The sky was a liquid blue, and Skinny could feel the warmth of the sun through an opening in the leafy canopy above him. He shifted his weight and heard a sound—the bubbling of running water. Bit by bit, Skinny eased himself up on his elbows.

Through the leaves glinted water—a little creek tumbling over stones. As Skinny struggled to his feet, his knees buckled, pain shot through his legs, and he fell. He groaned. His hand brushed something from his face. It was a feather, a black feather, and as he touched it Skinny felt softness and a vague memory. Painfully, he got up and limped through a tangle of dogwood, hepatica, and stalks of Indian pipe to the stream. Skinny knelt and plunged his head into the water. The coldness was delicious. Then he drank long and noisily. The water was clear and incredibly sweet. Skinny lay back and sighed with pleasure. Though his legs still throbbed, the ache in his head was gone and things came into focus. Skinny recalled the shadow that had descended and clutched him. Yes! It *had* clutched him! Who had brought him here, friend or foe?

He lay for some time, stretched out on his back, sorting out his thoughts. He definitely felt safe and relaxed. He had seen Ida again. The race through the tracts, the van, the lake. His escape by boat. Images crowded his brain, and he crawled into the creek, stretching out in it, tossing water over himself.

Out on the bank, he let his eyes roam among the sun-streaked branches of the jack pines. Gradually, he became aware of a pattern amid the limbs. The longer he stared, the more the pattern defined itself into a shape. A shape with two lights. Skinny felt a shiver. They were eyes, riveted on him. As Skinny pulled himself up, the owl seemed to float out of the foliage, and noiselessly descended to a bush, where he sat unblinking.

As Skinny stared at the owl he heard a voice. It spoke words Skinny could understand. It came from the owl, and Skinny never questioned it.

You are a kid, the voice said. *You must be a friend of Big Alice. I took you from the long ones. I brought you to Big Alice's home. But she is not here.*

The bird hooted three, low, melancholy notes that gave Skinny goosebumps.

Where is Big Alice?

Skinny murmured: "Big Alice is . . . sleeping. She's sick. The teachers have got her locked up somewhere at Scratchland."

The owl clacked his beak angrily. He flew to another branch, tore at a leaf, and shredded it, never taking his eyes from Skinny.

Skinny whispered, "You saved my life."

The bird bobbed his head.

Slowly, Skinny reached out his hand and placed a finger on the wicked-looking talons and stroked them.

Dig at the stump, ordered the owl.

Skinny brushed away twigs and leaves and uncovered a large stone. He lifted it and found a knapsack buried in shallow loam. A rough *A* was cut into one of the straps. Skinny excitedly rummaged in the bag. One by one, he drew out a cache of useful items: a ball of twine, matches, a dandy jackknife, a compass, a pencil, a note pad, a homemade rope ladder, a pair of binoculars, and a flashlight.

As Skinny was examining these things with delight, Hooter flew off. He soon returned with a flapping fish in his talons. He dropped it at Skinny's feet. Hooter did this three times. Quickly, Skinny scooped out a hole and filled it with rocks. He piled twigs over the stones and made a small fire. He laid the fish over the fire on a grill of green twigs. When they were baked, Skinny devoured them, heads, tails, all but the bones. The owl watched.

After his meal, Skinny leaned against a tree trunk. Closing his eyes, Skinny felt the warmth of the sun on his eyelids and a pleasant breeze on his face. The War was over, Skinny thought. Wouldn't it be wise to remain here at the preserve, safe for a while?

"Teachers need to have *one real kid* around." The remark Miss Bambi Dunphy had made to Ida came back to him, and he felt ashamed. If indeed he was a real kid, Skinny had no right to desert Big Alice, Curly, Fritzi, Barley, and the other kids who were now solidified into Young People. "But what can I do?" Skinny asked himself.

10

A Surprise

Three hoots woke Skinny.

Rudy is here.

"Who's Rudy?"

The owl bobbed his head and snapped his beak several times.

"I don't understand," said Skinny.

He is here now.

The bushes parted, and Skinny saw an animal the size of a wolf. He walked with his neck held stiffly to one side. There was a crooked smile on his face adding to a clownish appearance.

Rudy, said Hooter, *this is Big Alice's friend. The one called Skin-nee.*

Rudy sat on his haunches and examined Skinny.

Where is Big Alice?

Skinny was no longer surprised to find himself understanding what the animals said. He slowly and quietly explained to Rudy what had happened to Big Alice.

Rudy circled Skinny and sniffed. Skinny looked at the owl, but Hooter said nothing.

Rudy thrashed his tail. *The trap grows and grows.* He stopped before the knapsack and nudged it with his snout. *Use Big Alice's eyes,* he said and slunk off to sit under a bush a few yards away.

Skinny fished his hand into the knapsack. His fingers closed on the binoculars. He strung them around his neck and began to climb the nearest tree. Three-quarters of the way up he found a long, horizontal limb, which he slid across till he reached a place he could straddle comfortably.

To the west lay Lake Cachuma. The field glasses were so powerful, he could see individual cattails growing along its banks. Skinny swung the binoculars along the shoreline. There was no sign of human habitation until he spotted a splendid yacht anchored at a small dock at the northern end. Skinny trained his glasses on the ship for a full minute without seeing anyone. Then he focused on the flag flying from the stern, a large red *F* emblazoned against a black background. Skinny's chest tightened, making it difficult for him to breathe. He saw a mansion half hidden in trees, which he knew must be Mr. Foreclosure's summer house. There was no sign of life. Behind the house and beyond grew acre upon acre of virgin wilderness. Skinny gulped. An ugly swathe of fallen trees and stumps lay like a slash through the forest.

"So many trees cut down," Skinny murmured.

The owl's eyes bore in on him. *That is the Place Where Nests Fall. We are part of the War,* he said.

Again Skinny took up the binoculars, avoiding the plague spot. Skinny focused on what looked like an extensive garden behind the house, a rose garden. Surrounding it was a tall hedge of bushes, trimmed so peculiarly that Skinny stared in puzzlement. His stomach turned. The bushes, about eight to ten feet high, appeared to be insects. Yes the bushes were a topiary garden in the shapes of *insects!* There was something moving at the base of one bush. Coming up like a gopher from the earth was . . . a kid?

Skinny almost fell off his perch. A kid! No mistake

about that! A boy! First, two feet in sneakers without socks, followed by a pair of ragged shorts, then a torso wearing a torn sweat shirt. There were words on the back of the sweat shirt. Skinny smiled as he read:

UP WITH WORMS

11

Four Eyes

Bookworms are born with library cards in their hands. Turning pages is all they ever want to do. When they finish a book they can't wait to get to another.

Bookworms are not very popular. They bring books to the table at breakfast, lunch, and dinner, and their parents give them no peace. Bookworms must identify what they put in their mouths or parents aren't happy. It's a terrible struggle to get that book put down and closed. Sometimes a compromise is worked out, where a Worm eats with the book in his or her lap, but that's a constant irritation to everyone, especially to the Worm, who gets a food stain on a crucial word and has to backtrack a paragraph or two to figure out what that word was.

Bookworms need quiet places where no one bothers them. A kid named Four Eyes had found such a place, a culvert, where he sat and read. When he finished his book and had nothing else to read, he did some exploring. It was a dry time of year, and Four Eyes was able to go a long way into the culvert, even where it was too dark to read. Four Eyes started reading about culverts and conduits and waterways, and with a bunch of friends he located all the major culverts in his neighborhood.

It wasn't long before many Bookworms snatched their meals off the table and ran out with them into the drains and conduits. There, in the cool sewers, it was blissful reading with no nagging voices to jar them out of their stories. They were knee-deep in text and it was heaven.

What followed was quite natural. Long before Skinny's war, Bookworms found places underground where they could hide for days at a time, so long as they brought enough food and books. Soon Worms everywhere went down the drains. They stayed down for longer and longer periods of time, until they got permanently "lost" and no one could find them. Not one teacher or one parent ever found out where these kids went.

Sewers present certain problems, but the Worms found which sewer pipes were driest, lightest, which were the quietest, which were the most neglected by workers. They found places to sleep, places to hide food, and places to meet other Worms and trade books. The Worms even worked out a communications system, tapping messages on the walls or pipes, just as the Count of Monte-Cristo did. One drawback was slime and smell, but the Worms got used to both. When you're grazing, so to speak, in the fresh, lush grass of a new chapter by your favorite writer, you don't care how dirty you are or how bad things smell.

Bookworms generally had been a source of irritation to other kids in school because they tended to be teachers' pets. When they started disappearing there were many sighs of relief from the other kids. But to Skinny, with only an owl and a hyena to talk to, the prospect of seeing any kid, even a Bookworm, was overwhelming. Skinny was in a fever to find whoever had burrowed out of the earth before his eyes.

Rudy refused point-blank to accompany Skinny to

the rose garden, but Hooter reluctantly agreed to guide him there by air.

You are seeking the trap, said the owl.

"I've got to go!" cried Skinny. "There's a kid over there and I've got to find him!"

It was long, hard, arduous going for Skinny, under bushes and through tangles, stopping every now and then to listen. The forest was ominously silent. The shadow of the great owl preceded Skinny like a small storm cloud, sending squirrels and titmice scurrying into their holes.

After an hour, Skinny came to a barbed wire fence, eight feet tall. Beyond it loomed the weird bushes Skinny had seen through his binoculars.

Hooter circled the area warily, and then he landed. *I see nothing that will hurt you,* he said.

Skinny searched along the bottom of the fence for a way of crawling under it. Soon he found a place where a sharp incline ran beneath the fence, and he wiggled through. The neatly clipped bushes rustled, trailing long shadows over the red-haired boy like so many flags. He examined the bushes carefully. He went from one to another.

The bush he now stood in front of was shaped like two ants in combat. One ant had severed its adversary's head and was holding it in a mandible, while its legs clutched the lower body of its assailant. Farther down the gravel lane, Skinny saw a bush of an ant astride a writhing worm. Next to that was a leafy representation of an ant dismembering a butterfly. Skinny shuddered.

Then he heard a tapping noise. Skinny knelt beside a bush growing in a large, scooped-out pan of earth. A pool of water lay about its roots. A trickle coursed out of a crack in the shallow depression and zigzagged into an enormous black pipe half sunk in a pile of debris. Skinny studied the pipe and he heard the tapping noise again. It came from inside the pipe. He looked back at Hooter, who sat in the shadows of a tamarack tree.

Skinny poked his head into the pipe. A shallow

stream of water, a few inches deep, gurgled along a culvert about four feet in diameter. The round roof dripped with moisture, and Skinny's flashlight picked up something floating in the water. It was a shoelace. Skinny bent his head and, holding his flash steady, went forward into the pipe and picked up the shoelace. Had there been a kid in the pipe recently? Skinny went a bit farther into the pipe. It seemed to turn, and the roof became higher. Skinny stood up straight. The air was lighter. The dying sunlight shone through hundreds of cracks in the ceiling. The flashlight hung limp in his hands, forgotten. He heard the tapping noise, louder, now—and singing! A boy's voice, singing:

> A schoolroom is a dead place,
> Dead as dead can be.
> First it killed my brother,
> Now it's killing me.
>
> All are dead who teach there,
> All are dead who preach there,
> The only thing to learn there
> Is never to return there.

"Hey!" Skinny shouted. "Hey! Where are you?" He heard only the echo of his own voice.

Then, a few yards in front of him, a boy stood in the musty light. He was dressed in the ragged sweat shirt Skinny had seen through his binoculars and threadbare shorts. No socks, and sneakers with laces missing. From top to toe this kid was upholstered with bits and pieces of leaves, scraps of paper, twigs, and an indistinguishable mishmash of whatever finds its way down drains. Skinny stared hardest at the dirty eyeglasses. They were fingermarked, flecked with grains of mud, crisscrossed with scratches, and barely held together with rubber bands and straight pins. A sack strapped over the boy's back was loaded with books.

The two stared at each other.

Behind the glasses sparkled a pair of blue eyes. The glasses bridged a delicately formed nose above a mouth set in a perpetual **V**. His grin was irresistible. Skinny started to laugh, and the other joined him.

"I haven't seen a kid from the outside world in a long time. I'm Four Eyes."

"I'm Skinny."

"How'd you find this place?"

Skinny described how he'd spotted Four Eyes through his binoculars and then his discovery of the drainpipe.

"Humph! Gotta be more careful. C'mon to my place."

Skinny followed Four Eyes further down the pipe. After a few minutes, Four Eyes raised his arm, giving a right-turn signal.

They entered a new tunnel which was quite dry. The sides were made of heavy, jagged rocks, but the earthen floor was very smooth.

"No water here because we're on higher ground."

Four Eyes stopped at a recess covered by a large Indian blanket. He raised the blanket and gestured to Skinny to enter.

There were some deck chairs, shabby pillows, a rickety card table, a cot, and several stacked crates holding food and books, piles and piles of books. Against the walls stood books piled six feet high in places. A great many were falling apart, their covers missing, warped and smutched with mildew. There were papers stuck in many of the books, papers filled with doodling, diagrams, and cobwebby handwriting.

Four Eyes beckoned Skinny to a chair and produced a candle which he lit with a rusty cigarette lighter. "It's gonna get real dark soon. Are ya hungry?" Without waiting for an answer, Four Eyes rummaged in the crates and came up with several sandwiches wrapped in foil. "I have access to school cafeterias," he said, handing Skinny a couple of sandwiches. He walked over to a wall where a dozen sheets of mimeograph paper were taped over each other and perused the top sheet. "Tomorrow at Mt. Kisco, hot dog with chocolate milk. Well. That'll be nice." Sitting in one of the ramshackle chairs facing Skinny, Four Eyes watched him eat. Suddenly he stared at Skinny. Four Eyes did a double take. "You're not Skinny *Malinky*, are you?"

Skinny wolfed down the sandwiches, nodding his head. Four Eyes, pouring him some milk from a thermos into a cracked cup, said, "You're quite a hero. You're famous. How did you get here?"

Skinny drank down the milk, even though it didn't taste too fresh, and described how he had escaped the Status Quo Solidifier. He described Big Alice's defeat and her fate, but kept the identity of Mr. Foreclosure to himself.

"We've heard of Big Alice," said Four Eyes, taking off his glasses, steaming them with his breath, and wiping them. When he put them back on, they looked as dirty as ever.

"She comes from here, from the preserve. Haven't you ever seen her?"

"This is a big place, believe me. And I'm not usually aboveground."

Skinny heard the tapping noise again.

Four Eyes reached for the candle and went further back into the cave, gesturing for his new friend to follow.

From the ceiling hung a pipe about two feet wide. Four Eyes pushed an empty box under the pipe with his foot and with his hand turned a metal rod projecting from the pipe. *Whoosh!* A flood of books poured into the box, filling it helter-skelter, so that it overflowed.

Skinny picked up one from the floor. Its cover read: *The New Physics*. Another was *Dead Parrots Can't Talk*. "Where do all these books come from?"

Four Eyes tidied up the pile and pushed the box into a corner. Then he took a soiled package of gum out of a pocket, offering a piece to Skinny. He flipped a thumb upwards towards the pipe. "It's a matter of airducts and

165

pipes creating a vacuum. And then creating an *unva-cuum*. Simple, really. First of all, I ought to explain that this tunnel is connected to another tunnel, and so forth. Also connected to all these tunnels, at right angles usually, are sewer pipes. For hundreds of miles. We Worms live quite comfortably in most of the tunnels, and we use the sewers as transportation. We canoe down the deeper ones, but most are wade-able."

"How many Worms are there?"

"A dozen around here, near Lake Cachuma. Spread all over there must be a hundred of us. We see each other to exchange books or tips about the menus of the week."

"Menus?"

"Yeah. At schools. We all keep in touch with our schools. Sort of sentimental, but eminently practical. My books come from the Virginia Road School library. My favorite library."

"Is that near here?"

"Oh no. 'Bout fifty miles due north."

"You mean, Four Eyes, these books come from fifty miles away?"

"Oh sure. It's a little problem in physics I worked out one day when I'd run out of reading material. Airflow and pressure. We just suck books off the shelves. We do it at night."

Four Eyes grinned and deposited his gum on an eyeglass bow. "It's a question of diverting airflow and upping pressure. We have the correct conditions for what I call the Literary Flush. At night, when library doors and windows are shut tight, we Worms turn knobs and jiggle handles and unscrew pipes, and siphon off the books. 'Course, we get some titles we don't care for, but nothing's perfect."

"You mean the books come down these pipes?"

"From vents and ducts. That's it. 'Course, I'm not the only Worm doing it. There's a Worm under every school who knows how to do it now, thanks to me, and we synchronize our watches and do it together. That way, there's books for everybody."

"How often do you do it, this Literary Flush?"

"Once a week."

"So that's why so many books are missing from school libraries! How long have you been here?"

"Going on three years, but I take trips. I go to the Canary Islands or Siberia or the Rain Forest. Lots of choices down here." Four Eyes laughed. "The Canary Islands is a big sewer down south. The water sings in the pipes, lots of chirping. Siberia is Scratchland, the coldest sewer of all. You gotta wear wraps. The Rain Forest is west of here, drippy. Always wear a hat there. The water level is high and you have to canoe. Then there's Muck City. It smells the worst of all. More garbage than anywhere else. I go there only twice a year. Lots of things floating around I can use, like wire and pieces of wood." Four Eyes moved on with his candle. "C'mon. I'll show you my dock."

"Do you ever get lost?"

"Not anymore. We have signs all around and we marked trails, so it's impossible to get lost for very long." The kids halted before the entrance to a huge pipe. Skinny noticed a catwalk running a foot above a black, fetid stream. Two rungs brought them to the catwalk. Skinny wrinkled his nose in disgust.

"You get used to it," said Four Eyes. "I never smell it anymore, except at Muck City."

Four Eyes drew Skinny's attention to a canoe tied nearby, bobbing up and down. "The water level is only five feet here, but further on it gets deeper. These sewers were built long ago. Not used anymore. Every once in a while we get into a newer sewer, and that's when we have to be careful. These old pipes and tunnels are Before Christ, B.C.'s, as we call 'em. The new ones are A.D.'s Active Duty. And we stay away from the A.D.'s."

A clanking noise startled Four Eyes. He glanced

back at Skinny and without explaining, turned, indicating that Skinny was to follow him. Only when the two kids were in Four Eyes's cave, eating day-old tuna fish sandwiches (from Georgia Shotbolt Elementary School), did Four Eyes break the silence. He looked sharply at Skinny.

"You said that Big Alice is paralyzed under a glass case at Scratchland, right?"

"Yeah. She's on exhibit."

"That noise you heard is a signal. It came from Tom Horowitz. He's at B.C. 4, *Daisy Miller*. He named his sewer pipe after a Henry James book. He's a nut on Henry James. Anyway, Tom's sending along a visitor. Guess who, Skinny?"

Skinny shook his head.

"It's Big Alice. Now what do you think of *that?*"

12

Alarming Events

At her best, Big Alice was a formidable sight. A day's travel through sewers had made her terrifying. Her bristly hair was patchy with dampness and caked with sludge. Her torn muumuu was fragrant with souvenirs. When she bolted out of the darkness, both kids stepped back in fright, throwing their arms defensively before their faces.

Skinny recovered quickly. "Big Alice! I thought you were done for!"

Big Alice rose from her knees. Breathing hard, she looked from Skinny to Four Eyes and back again. "That's right," she snarled. "And I was, thanks to you and your friends."

She jerked a clawlike finger at Four Eyes. "Who's he?"

"Four Eyes. He lives here."

Big Alice spat. Four Eyes flinched. "Another Worm. They all look alike." She shook herself, and drops of slime spattered on Skinny and Four Eyes. "What's to eat?" she asked.

Four Eyes silently handed Big Alice two sandwiches and an apple.

"I *hate* tuna fish!" she cried, throwing the sandwiches down. She smelled the apple, then popped it whole into her mouth and proceeded to noisily chew it up. "More! I want *more!*"

Four Eyes left and returned with more sandwiches—bologna. Big Alice swallowed them whole. Four Eyes made three more trips. (Frankly, Dear Reader, he was terrified.)

Skinny took a resolute step forward. He reached out and grabbed Big Alice's hand. "I'm glad you're here."

Big Alice stood stock-still. Strange to say, she was trembling.

Skinny went on in a very low voice: "We're all that's left, Big Alice. All the rest are solidified, except for the Worms down here." He paused. "You were terrific at the tournament. Everyone thought so."

Big Alice shook away Skinny's hand. She crumpled down on all fours. Not looking at Skinny, she muttered, "The Dumpys got me awake, took me to their house. I found a way out in a hole."

"A hole?"

"Yeah. In their basement."

Skinny hunkered down beside her. For a moment, neither spoke. All that could be heard was water dripping.

"The War isn't over," Skinny murmured.

Big Alice looked up at Skinny. "I know it isn't." She made a sound, half sigh, half growl. "Never over for me. Never over for you." Suddenly she cocked an ear. From above came an eerie sound, the song of a hyena. It was Rudy howling for his friend.

Big Alice rose. "I knew I was at Cachuma!"

Skinny nodded.

Big Alice rested a hand gently on Skinny's cheek.

"Has-ta ma-nā-na," she said, mispronouncing all the *a*'s.

She smiled and looked almost like a real girl. She put

170

her long, hairy arms around Skinny and pressed him roughly to her chest.

Then she was gone.

The next morning, Four Eyes served breakfast on an overturned barrel. There were several hard-boiled eggs, two hamburger buns (without hamburgers), peach halves encased in gelatin, and a bowl of fresh blueberries which Four Eyes had picked in the preserve that morning.

"I moved a log over the entrance, and loads of leaves, and planted some grape vines around it. Soon it will be invisible. No one will find me again."

"What about Mr. Foreclosure?"

"He doesn't care what's here at Cachuma. Schools and ants, that's all he cares about."

"*Ants,* Four Eyes?"

"That's right, ants. Mr. Foreclosure is supposed to be an authority on ants."

Silence.

"Have you ever been under his house, Four Eyes?"

"I been *in* his house. In his library. That is *one* library I don't want to snitch books from, believe me!"

"Why?"

"Too ghoulish."

"Take me there," said Skinny. "I have to go there."

"There's a lot of climbing through air ducts. It's not easy."

Skinny insisted, and finally Four Eyes led him to a stream of water cascading down one of the recesses. They took off their clothes and washed. Clean, Four Eyes was almost unrecognizable. They greased themselves with generous amounts of lard from a canister Four Eyes had stolen from a school kitchen.

They snaked their way into one pipe and out another, Skinny following close behind Four Eyes. Red arrows, crudely painted, were all the markings Skinny would remember later, but he would be sure to remember what he and Four Eyes overheard as they rested in a very tight air duct.

"We shall make the Cachuma Utility the most powerful institution of its kind on this planet." Skinny recognized the voice of Dr. Pucker, and clutched Four Eyes by the leg.

"The Cachuma Utility will be a laboratory for the most resourceful counterinsurgency techniques mankind can devise. We will channel our most talented teachers to it." The voice was small and raspy, and sent shivers up and down his spine.

"If anyone can do it, Mr. Foreclosure, you can," declared the voice of Dr. Pucker. Skinny's body turned icy cold. Four Eyes placed his finger on his lips.

"Thank you, Dr. Pucker. But nothing comes easy. Even the Status Quo Solidifier has produced unwelcome side effects."

"How so, sir?"

"The solidified kids are a most welcome addition to the ranks of erudition, wouldn't you agree, Dr. Pucker?"

Dr. Pucker must have nodded, for Mr. Foreclosure went on.

"And yet . . . because of solidification, hundreds of my factory workers will be thrown out of work, and I myself will stand to lose millions of dollars!"

"Is that possible?" This was the voice of Colonel Kratz.

"It is indeed! The solidified kids have lost their desire for sweets. My candy bar sales are down—75 percent this quarter! I've had to close eight of my bubble gum factories and all but one of my soda pop plants. The Young People all want to chew natural honeycomb and to drink skim milk. Unless I can devise a stopgap solution, my school-supply companies must declare bankruptcy!"

"Your school-supply companies?" echoed Dr. Pucker. "I don't understand."

Mr. Foreclosure made a thin, gravelly, snorting noise.

"Y.P.'s don't eat paste, steal chalk, bite down on pencils, use up erasers, or carve on desks. They write on both sides of a piece of paper. Ruinous, absolutely ruinous for me!" A sardonic little squeaking laugh was followed by the sound of papers rustling. "However, gentlemen, I am more than willing to pay such a price for the success of the Status Quo Solidifier. The fly in the ointment is Skinny Malinky."

Skinny's throat went dry and his heart began thumping madly.

"As long as he remains free and unsolidified, he is a threat to our plans, a threat we cannot afford to ignore. We know he is somewhere in this area. All witnesses agree he was snatched up by some huge, flying bird. Some say it was an eagle, some a vulture. Mrs. Solemnsides swears it was a pterodactyl.

"As you know, gentlemen, our largest organizations, the National Alliance of Teacher Cartels, the International PTA, and the Association for Holders of Advanced Degrees, will be sending representatives here in five days. Next Tuesday, to be exact."

Four Eyes touched Skinny on the shoulder.

"I sit as ex officio president on the executive boards of all these groups. Sterling, of course, remains my visible representative. While we meet here, schools all over the country will have simultaneous staff meetings, plugging in on the decisions we make here. Sterling will make three proposals. One: Skinny Malinky will be caught. Two: Six thousand football coaches with flamethrowers will parachute into Cachuma. They will burn off vegetation over a hundred-linear-mile area, and eight hundred personnel from military schools will penetrate the farthermost reaches of the preserve in tanks. Three: Our most prestigious teachers of electronics will solidify what is left standing."

"I don't quite follow your last statement, Mr. Fore-closure."

"To be sure, Dr. Pucker. We plan to use the Status Quo Solidifer on plants and animals, trees especially. Just between us, gentlemen, there are valuable mineral and oil deposits beneath our feet. Even if we fail to scare up Malinky, we will have opened up this region for *capital development.* You, my friends, will help us direct this inspiring operation!"

"Let us retire, please, to the game room for refreshment," said Sterling Guts.

The voices faded.

After they returned to Four Eyes's hideout, Four Eyes retreated to a corner with *Dead Parrots Can't Talk.* All Skinny's attempts to draw him into conversation failed. Four Eyes couldn't be reached. He read all day, and when night came he was still reading.

Skinny wandered up and down the sewer, plagued by the insidious voice of the ant, Mr. Foreclosure. He had to do something. He could not stay here.

Skinny worked his way out of the rubble piled at the culvert entrance and emerged into the cool, pleasant night air of the forest. He came face to face with Hooter, the great horned owl.

The bird swooped low, brushing the tip of his wing against Skinny's shoulder, and dropped something at his feet. It was a little oilskin sack. Inside was a coiled rope.

Raise your arms. Grab on to my legs, said Hooter.

Skinny closed his eyes, and with a great flapping of wings, the giant bird rose with his passenger and flew high over the treetops. Skinny finally opened his eyes. They were approaching a dark building. A tiny light shimmered from a third-floor window.

Hooter landed on the roof. *Go to the light. I will be here when you return.*

Skinny uncoiled the rope. Along the roof ran a low railing. He tied one end firmly to one of the rods and let himself down carefully to the lighted window. It was open, and Skinny swung himself into an immense room.

It was the library of Mr. Foreclosure.

13

A Ray of Hope

Skinny saw the paintings first. They were oil portraits in ornate, gold-leaf frames, horrible portraits, all of ant queens. There was a picture of a queen being bathed and brushed by workers. Another picture depicted a queen laying her eggs. The title read: *The Mother of Us All*. Still another painting showed a fat queen tearing open the cocoons from which workers emerged to serve and feed her. The most dramatic and beautifully rendered picture was of a winged queen mating in the air. The title beneath this painting read: *Apotheosis*.

Skinny walked down the oak floor, past a long table, past an antique desk, toward a figure at the end of the room, leaning over a table and dusting a large white lampshade.

Skinny stopped. It was incredible how happy and giddy he felt.

The figure turned and switched on the lamp. It was Ida.

She was wearing a uniform. She gave Skinny a quick smile, then went back to her dusting.

"Are you working for Mr. Foreclosure?"

"Yep," said Ida.

"Do you like it?"

"It got its good points."

After a minute, Skinny asked, "Can I help too?"

Ida tore her rag and handed half to Skinny, saying, "This here table needs a good wipe."

Skinny rubbed the table legs hard and briskly. "What's school like with all those Y.P.'s?"

"Oh, they polite all right. But you can't get past hello or good-bye with *them*. Blackboard too clean. Wastepaper too clean. Feet too clean. And those Y.P.'s know answers before teachers ask 'em. It different when you there, Skinny."

"Do you think the War's over, Ida?"

Ida spat on her cloth and rubbed something on the oak panel above her. "Your War don't end."

"I don't know what I can do now." Skinny found a bottle of polish under the table and poured some onto his cloth. "Mr. Foreclosure is going to kill the whole preserve and build some kind of awful Cachuma Utility."

Ida walked over to a large oak chair and began going over it with her rag. "What are you going to do about it?" she asked.

Skinny followed her about the room. She straightened one of the paintings on the wall and gazed at it, shaking her head. "That really somethin', that one! It make me want to scratch!"

"Ida, do you know this house real good?"

"From top to bottom. 'Specially bottom."

Skinny thought about this and then grinned and took Ida's hand. "Ida, you just gave me a fantastic idea!"

"Did I, Skinny?"

"Top to bottom, Ida! Top to bottom!" Skinny ran over to the window, placing a leg over the sill. "I gotta talk this idea over with my friend, Four Eyes. I wish you could come with me."

Ida touched the side of his face. "Don't matter. Me here, you there. We got each other's luck."

Skinny took the rope. "What about Mr. Foreclosure, Ida?"

"Someday, somebody step on him." The black eyes glistened.

Skinny swung himself out. He shinnied up to the roof, where Hooter was waiting. Together they soared into the air, and soon Skinny was dropped gently to the earth.

He was back in the cave when Four Eyes turned the last page of a book. Skinny rubbed his eyes. It was as if he had never left the cave.

"Four Eyes?"

"Yes? What is it? You look all riled up."

"The Literary Flush, how do you do it?"

"Yeah, what about it?"

Skinny's eyes were wide and his freckles snapped. "Could you make it bigger?" Skinny placed his hand on Four Eyes's shoulder. "*Bigger,* Four Eyes? So big that you could suck all the teachers in all the schools down into the deepest darkest sewers for ever and ever?"

You could almost see Four Eyes's mind shift gears. He stuck out his chin, took off his glasses, stared at them, put them on again. He chortled. "Possible. *Highly* possible!" Four Eyes rummaged in a pocket, took out a sheaf of wrinkled papers, smoothed them out, and studied them, muttering numbers and letters. His nostrils flared and his blue eyes danced. "Not just highly possible but *workable!*"

The kids grabbed each other.

"How many days, Skin, do we have?"

"Five days. Next Tuesday. There's a meeting here at Mr. Foreclosure's house and it's going to be hooked up to schools everywhere."

"I have to call an emergency meeting of the Worms. Can't do it without their help."

"Will they do it?"

Four Eyes blinked and pressed his lips together. "They've *got* to do it, Skinny."

14

The Congress
of Worms

Along the sides of a monstrous sewer pipe ran a series of thinner pipes, some with knobs projecting at odd angles. On these pipes and knobs perched a mass of Worms, perhaps sixty or seventy-five in all. They were of various ages and sizes and incredibly scruffy. They all had books open on their knees.

Four Eyes had brought his companions together by means of the elaborate pipe-tapping codes. The Worms had resisted at first, grumbling at the interruption of their favorite books. ("Favorite" being, Dear Reader, *any* book in which a Worm is presently engrossed.) It took all night, but they assembled by morning. After all, it was an opportunity to trade books.

A great amount of haggling took place. "I'll trade you my *Just So Stories* for your *East of the Sun and West of the Moon*," or "I'll give you four Martha Finleys for two E. Nesbits," and so forth.

Four Eyes, in desperation, had to take strong measures to bring the meeting to order. He held up a book and slowly began tearing out a page. Everyone froze. As Four Eyes continued to tear the page, several voices shouted, "Stop! Stop it!"

Four Eyes held up the torn page before the horrified Worms. "It's okay. It's only the title page from *Robert's Rules of Order.*"

A sigh of relief issued from the group. One Worm grumbled, "I *like* reading *Robert's Rules of Order.*" She was shushed.

"I called this meeting to introduce my friend, Skinny Malinky, and to tell you some important news. I know some of you have heard of Skinny."

"Sure," replied a pimply Worm at the top of the pipe, without raising an eye from Palgrave's *Golden Treasury.* "He organized and led the last War against the Teachers."

One or two Worms placed bookmarks between their pages, looking curiously at Skinny.

Four Eyes directed his words to these Worms, who, Skinny suspected, were highly respected. Four Eyes spoke for at least twenty minutes. He told the Worms all that Skinny had related to him, and finished with a description of what he and Skinny had overheard in the air duct next to Mr. Foreclosure's library.

Most of the Worms hadn't bothered to look up from their books. Skinny bit at his fingers, feeling discouraged.

A fat Worm who had been reading *Principia Mathematica* called down, "Foreclosure is a capitalist pig. If he drills here for oil, we're sunk."

"Oh come off it, Smudge," jeered Tom Horowitz, the pimply Worm, "let's not have another sermon."

A Worm named Itchy piped up: "Mr. Foreclosure is a threat to the animals. I've seen two badgers, one raccoon, and a wolverine with cubs in my sewer."

Many Worms stopped reading.

"The animals of the preserve are frightened," said one.

"It has nothing to do with us," said Tom Horowitz, disgustedly closing his book. "We can't afford to make any dumb moves. I live under Scratchland, and it's been real quiet since the Kids have been solidified, and that's okay with me."

Several Worms scowled.

"I agree with Itchy," exclaimed Smudge. Smudge leaned towards a Worm who wore rings on all his fingers and was reading *Eight Plays of the Restoration*. "What do you say, Jigger? You're the animal expert."

Jigger twisted a ring slowly. "The animals are in a bad way. And so are we." He banged his book shut. All the readers now quietly closed their books. Jigger looked eagerly at Skinny. "What do you want us to do, Skinny?"

"Four Eyes showed me how you Worms get your books. Couldn't you do the same thing on a bigger scale? Flush the Teachers?"

A smile radiated across Smudge's face. "Shades of Nicodemus!" he cried. "That is something to conjure with!"

The Worms hummed and buzzed.

Four Eyes raised his hand. "In five days teachers will be meeting in schools everywhere. Here at Lake Cachuma, there'll be a hotshot gathering of the most important teachers in the world. They're going to push through a decision to raze and gut the preserve—in the name of security. That means we may get solidified."

Tom Horowitz rose. All eyes were on him.

"There's always been wars against teachers. And there always will be. Granted, Mr. Foreclosure is evil, but even if he died, someone else would take his place. Malinky is fighting a lost cause." Tom spoke in a staccato voice that rang throughout the pipe. "So what if we can flush the Teachers and Mr. Foreclosure's brain trust into the sewers? Who wants 'em down *here*? This is where we *live*, where we *read*! I don't want to ever have to bump into my old English teacher down here! Do *you*?"

A Worm sitting behind Tom Horowitz cried out, "Not me! And I frankly couldn't care less about what happens to the kids on the outside. Boob-tubers, that's what they are! They deserved what they got!"

There were many nods of agreement. Skinny's heart sank.

"Flush 'em into Muck City," yelled Itchy. "That'll be *terminal*, believe me!"

Smudge rose, facing Tom Horowitz. "Don't you see, you thickhead, that this is what we've been waiting for? If the teachers are all down here, we can get back into the world! No teachers to tell us *what* to read and *when!*"

"You mean . . . leave the sewers?" asked a Worm named Andromeda McKutchin. The book on her lap was titled *Nefertiti and the Role of Women in Egyptian History*.

"Yes, you cretin!" shouted Smudge. "I hate moldy egg salad sandwiches!"

Tom was climbing down from his perch. When he reached the catwalk, he turned and said, "I'm not having any part of this. Count me out."

"We decided it was one for all and all for one—right, Worms?" called Four Eyes.

Many nodded.

"If you leave, Tom, you can't be part of us again. That means no book trading."

Tom turned pale. He faced the group. "Let's put it to a vote!"

"All right," said Jigger, standing. He was short, with a big nose and misshapen ears, but his face was alive with intelligence. The Worms listened carefully.

"I just want to say one more thing. I know how Tom feels. It's hard to stop reading. I don't ever want to. And I don't have any great sympathy for the Boob-tubers. I'd just as soon wait down here until they become extinct. But we're kids too, even though we're Worms. And kids like Skinny have been fighting for *me*."

"Why doesn't he become a Worm, then!" cried a voice.

"That's not the point. Kids should be what they want to be. Skinny has a right to do what he wants to do. But Tom's wrong about this being just another war. It's not." Jigger paused. "It's the *last* War. I know it because I can see how the animals behave. There are fewer and fewer animals left. Fewer and fewer preserves left. Back of Lake Cachuma is Brummagem Forest. It may be the last wilderness left, not even on maps because the man who surveyed it for Mr. Foreclosure conveniently disappeared. I've done a lot of research on this Mr. Foreclosure. He's too rich and too powerful. After he solidifies the world, he'll go after the moon and the stars. If we Worms flush him and all his teachers down to Muck City, we can come out of our holes and take over. And it's about time, I say."

Four Eyes called, "How many Worms *against* supporting Skinny and the Grand Flush?"

A few hands went up along with Tom's.

"How many *for* the Grand Flush?"

It was an overwhelming majority. Tom and his supporters stalked out.

Itchy waved an arm frantically.

"What is it, Itchy?" asked Four Eyes.

"What about Miss Edwards?"

"What do you mean?"

"I mean that I don't want Miss Edwards from Virginia Road School flushed! She was the best teacher I ever had!"

Now many of the Worms looked concerned.

"I don't want Mrs. Burroughs at Vineland flushed down," said another Worm.

"Or Mrs. Garrison, either!" cried another.

"Or the Dunphy sisters at Scratchland," added Skinny.

"We can work that out," said Four Eyes.

"We'll parcel out jobs right now," said Jigger. "Some

of us will contact those teachers we want saved. Some will work on the Flush. There's a lot to do."

The Worms began swarming down the sides of the pipe, books in hand, and Jigger came up to Skinny.

"We've got to help you, Skinny," he said, and his large eyes were warm. "There's no other way."

15

Preparations

The Worms were busy. The pipes, ducts, and vents under hundreds of schools had to be adjusted so teachers would not be flushed into sewers already inhabited by Worms but would be routed into Muck City. Muck City was the most fetid and convoluted sewer of all. Worms had avoided it ever since Dougie Kilbourn had set up housekeeping there and was never seen again.

Smudge's crew drafted warnings and put them in sealed envelopes marked "Personal," addressed to those teachers the Worms had decided to spare. These envelopes were placed in teachers' mailboxes beside their rest-room keys. Skinny didn't sign his note to the Dunphy sisters but merely drew a picture of an ant at the bottom with an *X* over it. He knew the sisters would understand.

Four Eyes had spent almost two full days creeping and crawling under the Foreclosure house and inside its walls. When he'd finished, he said, "Skinny, there's a drain in Mr. Foreclosure's wine cellar that's crucial if we want to tie Foreclosure into the Grand Flush."

"We do. We do," said Skinny.

"Well, I sneaked down there and found that someone had beaten me to it. Taken off the drain cover. What do you think of that?"

Skinny mulled it over, and suddenly he grinned and nodded. "That's good, Four Eyes."

"Do you know who did it?" asked Four Eyes.

"Yes," said Skinny, and he touched the rabbit in his pocket.

The Worms made sure their own sewer pipes were out of the main path of the flood. So they could watch the Flush, they drilled peepholes along the main pipe that carried refuse to Muck City. Four Eyes and Jigger were chosen to sit at "Master Control," a place along the pipe where dozens of other pipes joined it. There, on a plank supported by two ladders, Four Eyes and Jigger would turn a series of knobs to create a vacuum in hundreds of pipes. Turning other knobs would activate this vacuum. The result would be the Grand Flush. Even though Four Eyes had worked it all out on paper and explained it a dozen times, it remained incomprehensible to everyone but himself and Jigger. Yet no one doubted that he could pull it off.

When zero hour was approaching, the Worms began settling themselves at their stations, reinforced by sandwiches, cold drinks, and a goodly supply of printed matter. Skinny sat with Four Eyes and Jigger on the narrow platform.

"Want some leftover shepherd's pie, Skinny?"

"No thanks, Four Eyes."

Jigger consulted an old pocket watch. "Three minutes to go," he said.

All down the line speech ceased. More than one Worm broke out in a cold sweat.

And then a strange whistling could be heard inside the pipe.

"That's *it!*" cried Four Eyes, and he turned one knob clockwise and another counterclockwise. Jigger did the same. For ten seconds nothing happened. Then the entire sewer shook, and with a loud *roomph!*—as if a

186

dam had burst somewhere over their heads—the pipe came alive with a hundred explosions.

The kids glued their eyes to the peepholes.

"What are those, torpedoes?" asked Jigger.

"Nope. They're wine bottles," replied Four Eyes. "Mr. Foreclosure's private stock."

"Wowie! They look like squadrons of bombs!" yelled Jigger.

"Here comes everything!" shouted Four Eyes.

16

Disaster!

The most famous teachers in the world had come to the special meeting at Mr. Foreclosure's summer home at Lake Cachuma. They were educators or fellows or professors, or doctors of this and doctors of that. You could play Scrabble with the letters that clung to their names. Fred Truncheon, for instance, was one of the most important educators. He was a Harvard A.P.A. (Associate of Perfect Attendance) and a Yale M.S.A. (Master of Seating Arrangements). Then there was Elvira Gertlestone, grand old lady of the Back to Basics movement, who held a degree in Suspensions and Expulsions and another in Whirlwind Reaping. There were a dozen other great names gathered in Mr. Foreclosure's oak-paneled library.

In one corner of the room, Guts stood conversing with Fred Truncheon.

"Our solidification program, Mr. Guts, is running well ahead of expectations."

"Good. Mr. Foreclosure will be glad to hear that. But are all the technical details on today's broadcast worked out?"

"Quite. It will be closed-circuit to the hundreds of

key schools whose staffs are congregating now, as we are. Very exciting."

"Excellent." Guts's voice fell a few decibels. "Can you tell me, Fred, about today's quotation?"

"At the closing of the market at 3 P.M. New York time, sir," Truncheon whispered, "Foreclosure Industries International rose to a gross market value of two hundred billion dollars."

"Wonderful! Wonderful! And what is your figure for those kids who had 'accidents' in the faulty solidifiers?"

"Only sixty-eight last week, Mr. Guts. They've all been successfully converted into breakfast cereal."

"Thank you, Fred. The Board will be pleased with your report."

Truncheon beamed.

The group now took places at the oak table, seating themselves in carved chairs which had been shipped to Cachuma from a twelfth-century château in France.

Sterling Guts rose. (Did he twitch because Mr. Foreclosure was behind his ear?) "Ladies and gentlemen, this is an auspicious occasion. At this very moment, on closed-circuit TV, the staffs of hundreds of schools are convened and listening to us. What we decide today will be momentous for the future of Young People." Guts then introduced each member of this prestigious committee. Minutes ticked by. Once, Sterling Guts heard slight noises which he attributed to Dr. Truncheon's annoying habit of grinding his dentures. (This noise, as you would suspect, Dear Reader, emanated from behind the library wall.)

Countless reports were delivered and accepted. Some forty minutes had passed, and the educators were deeply involved, when Mr. Guts said, "Now Miss Gertlestone, please. What has been the result of your committee's work with the Electric Tables project?"

Those were the last words spoken at this historic gathering in Mr. Foreclosure's library at Lake Cachuma.

It was as if a giant vacuum cleaner sucked everything down to the cellar from the top floor. The force was so strong it yanked pictures off walls. The door of a safe was pried open by the pressure, and thousands of hundred-dollar bills whizzed through the house. Miss Gertlestone was trying to snatch as many of these bills as she could, twisting her body in the air like a contortionist.

Sterling Guts had the presence of mind to cling to an ancient stone flambeau projecting from the wall. From there he was able to propel himself into Mr. Foreclosure's massive vault. In the nick of time, he closed the iron door, thereby saving himself and his employer from the powerful suction which lifted everyone and everything else into the air and down the long staircase.

Down, down into the sewers spun almost the entire Executive Board of the National Alliance of Teacher Cartels.

17

The Grand Flush

"Who's the guy broncobusting the umbrella?" asked Skinny.

"That's Fred Truncheon, one of the slimiest teachers alive," said Four Eyes.

Truncheon indeed was perched atop his opened umbrella, holding on for dear life. A swarm of Class A stock certificates escorted him through the pipe.

"Which one is Mr. Foreclosure?" asked Jigger.

"Don't know," answered Four Eyes.

Skinny climbed down from the platform and ran several yards to another group of peepholes, around which were clustered other Worms.

"Look!" screamed Itchy. "There's old Mrs. Hazeltine on top of her desk!"

"No kidding!" cried another. "I had her for geography. She said I didn't know my latitude from my longitude."

The Worms yelled with excitement on recognizing teachers and principals. Those schools nearest the preserve were now being emptied. The sewer roared. On and on the whirlwind flew!

"Who's the man talking into the telephone?" asked one Worm.

"He's my old principal at Lockjaw Avenue, Mr. Bloatum! And there's his secretary holding on to a typewriter!"

Through the pipe they came, thick and fast, in twos, threes, and in clusters, interspersed with TV sets. Teachers who had never said more than a muffled "Good morning" to one another now clung together, terror-stricken. Many teachers had taken the correct Emergency Drop drill position, knees tucked against belly, chins on chest, and were transported in this position all the way down to Muck City.

Twenty minutes later, teachers were still being sucked through the sewer, but some Worms had become bored. They opened books and began to read.

"Maplewood School coming up!" shouted one Worm. All the Worms who'd gone to Maplewood closed their books.

"Excelsior Avenue School!" cried another.

And so it went.

The Worms closest to Muck City later said that the horror on the teachers' faces would always be remembered.

"Hey!" exclaimed a Worm. "There goes Maplewood School *again!* What's going on?"

"Mr. Bloatum just went by the *other* way!" said another Worm.

It was true. Before the Worms' astonished eyes, the staffs of the schools were reversing, being sucked *back!*

"What's going on!" There were cries of outrage, surprise.

Skinny raced over to Master Control, where Jigger was struggling with Tom Horowitz. Tom was fighting to hold Jigger away from the control. Four Eyes lay in a heap beneath the trestle, his head bleeding. Skinny grabbed Tom by his ankles and toppled him. Together, Jigger and Skinny easily subdued him.

Four Eyes sat up and shook his head from side to side. Skinny knelt before him.

"Jigger! Turn the knobs back before it's too late!"

Jigger leaped up to the platform and madly twiddled the knobs. There were shouts of "Hurray! They're coming back again!"

Four Eyes sighed, took out a large, dirty handkerchief, and wiped the blood from his forehead.

The kids turned to Tom Horowitz. He sat scrunched in a heap, tears streaming down his face. "You'll be sorry. You'll be sorry," he croaked. Then he shakily got up and disappeared down the catwalk.

"Let him go, Skinny," said Jigger from above. "He hasn't any more harm in him."

As Skinny and Four Eyes climbed back onto the trestle, he added, "Tom's set himself a real hard goal, and he's afraid that if he gets drawn into the War he'll never be able to finish it."

"What's that?" asked Skinny.

"He's reading all the novels of Henry James."

"What's so hard?" remarked Four Eyes. "He did that last year."

"Yeah, but not in cuneiform, he didn't."

"What's cuneiform?" asked Skinny.

"It's old Persian writing. Wedge-shaped characters," replied Jigger. "Tom's read Henry James for years. Last month he decided to start all over again. Only he's going to translate them first into cuneiform." He sighed. "Tom's always been different."

After ten minutes, nothing was coming through the sewer except paper towels and a shining, whirling cloud of jumbo paper clips.

"That's it," said Four Eyes. He and Jigger turned the knobs again. The roaring stopped. Clanking. Slamming. "Doors closing," Four Eyes murmured. Then the sound of a wind dying down. And silence.

The three kids shook hands. Cheers could be heard up and down the line.

"We done it," said Four Eyes. "The rest, Skinny, is up to you."

18

A Talk

Skinny moved up the grand circular driveway to the front entrance of Foreclosure's house. His feet crunched on the gravel. The mahogany door swung perilously from one hinge, and Skinny entered the main hall. The house was a shell. The wealth which had adorned each room had vanished into the sewers.

Ida stood at the foot of the stairs, squeezing a mop over a bucket.

Skinny studied her. She looked exactly as she had when he first met her years before, in the kindergarten room at Ripley Street School.

"You work too hard, Ida."

"Well, I done here now." She went to a small closet and deposited the bucket and mop in a corner.

"I'll be leaving Cachuma soon," said Skinny.

"I 'spect so. Miss Jenny and Miss Bambi be happy to see you again. They got good hearts." She took an old, threadbare coat from the closet and put it on.

"Ida?"

"What, Skinny?"

"Did we win the War?"

"You come close, Skinny." Ida walked to the front

door. She stopped and turned to Skinny. "You done what you had to do. Rest of the pieces fall in place."

"Ida?"

"What, Skinny?"

"You make me feel happy."

Ida smiled, placed four fingers to her lips, then extended her hand to him.

Skinny was very tired. He sank down on the beautiful floor and stretched out. The little carousel in his head began going round and round.

19

Liberation

Skinny and Four Eyes, along with eight other Worms, arrived at Scratchland at four o'clock the next Saturday afternoon. They found empty offices, empty classrooms.

Four Eyes and Skinny, with the Worm named Andromeda McKutchin, scouted the area while the rest of the party sat on the empty cafeteria floor.

Andromeda still wore the retainer and headgear she had been wearing when she ran away from home two years before. She used it to clip messages to herself, such as *Look up* Narnia *in* Oxford English Dictionary and *The word behind the apple butter stain on page 79 of* Little Princess *is* indiscretion. The retainer, with its dangling papers, gave her an official surgical appearance. Nothing she said was ever taken lightly.

When they got to the library, Andromeda groaned. The papers on her head strap shivered. "Oh no!"

"What is it?" said Four Eyes.

"The shelves are empty!"

"Of course. The books have all been sucked down into Muck City. We'll fill 'em up again."

Four Eyes and Andromeda unloaded their backpacks and lovingly placed their books on the bare shelves.

Andromeda squinted at one of the titles. "Hey, Four Eyes, can I borrow your *Tale of Two Cities?*"

"Sure, if you'll let me read your *Père Goriot.*"

"Can't. I've seven more chapters to go. How about *The Mysterious Island* instead?"

"I've read that three times already, but that's okay, I'll read it again."

Suddenly Skinny stiffened. Faces were peering through the windows. A gang of kids stood in the doorway.

A muscular kid wearing a T-shirt that said Long Live Bubble Gum stepped forward. "Is it true that the teachers have all disappeared?"

"The bad ones, anyway," said Four Eyes.

The muscular kid introduced himself as Bax. He was obviously delighted to meet Skinny. "I heard about you for a long time. Glad to catch up with ya."

"Same here. How'd you kids escape the S.Q.S.?"

"We hid. Teresa, here, hid in a car wash for three days. I was in a funeral parlor."

"Are there very many kids who escaped the Solidifier?"

"A few, quite a few. No telling when they'll show up. Say, there's a lot of good stuff at the dump we could bring in here."

"Like what?"

"Like car seats, 'cause I don't see any chairs around here. Teresa is dying to build a drag strip, right, Teresa?"

Teresa flashed an exuberant smile. "Yeah. I'd like to get my '65 GTO in shape. We could build a quarter-mile track on the playground."

Andromeda McKutchin slammed her book shut with a bang and walked out of the room.

By Monday the kids had changed Scratchland into a comfortable place—for kids interested in cars. Most of the rooms looked like machine shops. Under the tutelage of Teresa, Bax and the others who had arrived with her were dismantling car bodies, replacing transmissions, and refitting fenders. A few Worms were researching technical problems for them. The rest of the Worms settled in the library. Scratchland was busy, loud, and greasy.

At eight o'clock, the Dunphy sisters drove into the school parking lot in their blue 1941 Hudson. They were quickly surrounded by cheering kids.

Miss Jenny took hold of Skinny's hand, and his face reddened to match his hair. "Oh, Skinny! We are so happy to see you safe. Aren't we, Bumpy dear?"

"Heavens, yes! I can't tell you how Jenny and I worried about you."

"Thank you for that lovely note but . . ." Miss Jenny looked slightly troubled. "I suppose you saved our lives. Are all the other teachers . . . gone, Skinny?"

"That's right, Miss Jenny," said Skinny, disengaging his hand from the teacher's impassioned clutch.

Four Eyes grinned. "Skinny said you were the best teachers at Scratchland. You saved Big Alice's life."

"Who might *you* be, young man?"

"I'm Four Eyes. A Worm. You've heard of Bookworms, haven't you?"

"Oh my *yes,*" exclaimed Miss Bambi, and she took out one of her slim cigars.

Andromeda McKutchin frowned and muttered, "That's a filthy habit."

Teresa had been examining the Dunphys' Hudson with admiration. "Say, would ya mind if I looked under the hood?" she asked.

"Of course not, dear."

"Oh, *fantastic!*" cried Teresa, plunging her head into the engine.

Bax, beside her, said, "The fan belt's cracking. And the radiator needs work."

Teresa, her face positively radiant, approached the Dunphys and, with a gentleness and respect in her voice that no one had heard before, asked, "I'd love to drive it. Do you think I could? I promise to bring her back soon. Could I please?"

Miss Jenny placed a palm on Teresa's cheek and smiled. "You certainly may." She looked at her sister.

Miss Bambi inhaled and nodded.

Fifteen minutes later, the Dunphys were sitting on two car cushions in the Scratchland library with Four Eyes, Skinny, and Andromeda McKutchin.

"Now, Skinny," said Miss Jenny, clearing her throat, "both Bambi and I want you to know how grateful we are that you kids warned us in time. But I must say, we are curious as to what we were warned *about*. What *did* you do with the rest of the teachers?"

"We flushed 'em down into the sewers, Miss Jenny," said Skinny.

The sisters stared at each other and gasped.

"Do you think they will survive?" asked Miss Bambi anxiously.

Skinny looked away. "They might," he muttered.

"As much as I sympathize with you kids," said Miss Jenny, "I believe it is important to be humane. The conqueror, as Marcus Aurelius said somewhere, must be generous or he does not deserve his victory."

Miss Bambi bobbed her head and flicked an ash.

"We left loads of food in Muck City. And life preservers," said Andromeda.

Skinny turned to Andromeda in astonishment. "You did?"

"Yes," replied Four Eyes. "I guess we Worms figgered the teachers ought to be given a 20–80 chance to survive."

"All their furniture and files went down with them, so the teachers ought to feel right at home," added Andromeda.

"Plus ditto machines and lots of paper," said Four Eyes.

Miss Jenny sighed. "Well, I suppose that's fair enough."

"What exactly, Skinny, do you have in mind for *us*?" asked Miss Bambi.

"Mechanical drawing might be an appropriate subject," murmured Miss Jenny. "We have so much to learn in that area, do we not, Bumpy, dear?"

"That's okay for *some* kids," exclaimed Andromeda, who sat well out of range of Miss Bambi's cigar, "but *I'm* not interested in mechanics or cars. It's stupid and a waste of time."

Four Eyes stirred uneasily. "Well, I guess I agree with Andromeda. And I know I speak for the other Worms here. I, personally, would like to examine in some depth the houses of E. Nesbit."

The Dunphys looked at each other in some bewilderment.

"Who is E. Nesbit, Four Eyes?"

"You mean, Miss Jenny, you never read E. Nesbit!"

Miss Jenny passed around a box of saltwater taffy. "Why don't you and Andromeda lead *us* in a practicum about this E. Nesbit? It sounds good to me. What did he write?"

"*She,*" declared Andromeda, chewing her taffy lustily.

Skinny, who had been standing near a window, suddenly interrupted with "Hey, look! There's a crowd of people in the yard! They're lining up!"

The sisters exchanged a look and rose. Miss Bambi put out her cigar. "The Y.P.'s," she muttered, and gazed out the window sourly.

Miss Jenny joined her. "What a sorry-looking lot they are."

The Y.P.'s were lining up for school, girls in one line, boys in another. There was no pushing, pulling, or talking. What distressed Skinny and his friends most was the way these former kids looked. They were dressed in suits, ties, neat dresses, and newly shined shoes. Each Y.P. carried a thick notebook, the cover embossed with the words *Scratchland Deportment*.

"They look like little old men and women!" cried Andromeda, wrinkling her nose in disgust.

"The effects of the Status Quo Solidifier," said Miss Jenny, and sighed. "It's quite sad."

"I believe, Skinny, you ought to go out and talk to them," said Miss Bambi. "They'll stay out there forever unless they receive permission to enter."

Skinny, Four Eyes, Andromeda, and the Dunphy sisters slowly walked out of the building.

The Y.P.'s stood stiffly at attention.

Skinny gazed helplessly at the Y.P.'s. He opened his mouth, but nothing came out. He turned in despair to Miss Jenny, who moved forward and cleared her throat. "I want all you Young People to listen carefully." She paused. "The War between the Teachers and the Kids has . . . has been culminated. Teachers have been . . . have been . . . ummm . . ." She turned to Four Eyes and whispered, "Would you say *removed?*"

"I would," Four Eyes whispered back.

"The Kids have won the War."

The faces of the Y.P.'s froze with shock. No one moved from his or her place.

"Skinny and his friends harbor no ill will towards you. They want to cooperate with you to . . . to . . . to what, Skinny?"

"To help run schools," said Skinny, having found his voice. "The way *you* want to." He looked pleadingly at the quiet lines of boys and girls. "You don't have to stand in two straight lines anymore. You can stand any way you *want* to. Right now."

The Y.P.'s did nothing. They looked puzzled.

Skinny grimaced horribly as he wheeled back to Four Eyes. "How can I make 'em understand, Four Eyes?"

"What about your friends, Skin? Are they here? Chops and Curly and Fritzi?"

Skinny's face relaxed. He yelled out, "*Barley! Barley Chops! Curly! Fritzi!* Are you there? Where are you?"

Silence.

Miss Jenny called out: "Bartholomew Chops!"

A figure stepped out of line to face Skinny.

"Anatole Winkler!" cried Miss Bambi in a martial voice.

Another figure, smaller than the first, stepped out of line.

"Fritzi Nissenbaum!" commanded Miss Jenny, and a third Y.P. moved out of the girls' line.

Bartholomew Chops looked enormous in a double-breasted suit. His eyes were dull in a face as gray and soft as putty. His huge feet were encased in neatly buckled galoshes. Curly looked like a tiny, tired dormouse. His once curly hair was slicked back into a cowlick, and his mouth drooped. Fritzi was unrecognizable in a matronly green polyester dress. All three Y.P.'s had a sharp worry crevice between their eyebrows.

Skinny walked haltingly towards them. The closer Skinny got, the more fearful his former friends became, and when Skinny stopped before them, they were pale and shaking.

Skinny grabbed Curly by the hand. "Curly! Don't you know me?"

Curly cringed. So did most of the other Y.P.'s nearby. Uttering a strange, throaty cry, Skinny turned and ran back into the building.

That night, Skinny and the Worms sat down to talk in the Scratchland furnace room.

Skinny hunched in a corner, biting at his nails.

Four Eyes held up a piece of paper. "This is a letter I recently got from Smudge," he said. "He's at Christina Rosetti School—that is, the Rossetti Circus School. I want to read it to you."

"Okay," said Skinny.

Dear Four Eyes,

I'm not used to writing. It's easier to tap things out. But it's been a while since we've seen each other and I wanted to give you some idea of how things are going here.

About two dozen unsolidified kids showed up and they're all hot on making TV commercials. Their leader is a kid named Wimpy Costello who's collected a lot of TV equipment. His mother makes ten thousand dollars every time she compares one roll of toilet paper with another on one minute of prime time. (We call her the Biffy Queen.) Anyway, he's sold the rest of the kids on turning the school into a TV station. He barely tolerates us Worms. We are good for nothing except to look up something in a book.

The Y.P.'s are really getting us down. They're so passive it hurts. Beezer Martin is here. Solidified. You should see him. All he thinks about are the knots of his ties. Some of us Worms decided to try to turn some of the Y.P.'s back into Kids. We tried experiments (harmless) on a select group. We force-fed them candy every two hours for two weeks. Not one pimple. We took away their combs, brushes, hair oil, toothpaste, soap. They never got dirty. We did get one Y.P. to pick his nose in public—that was our biggest achievement.

At any rate, as you might gather by now from the tone of this letter, we are generally disgusted. It's too noisy to read—too many interruptions. And the way the Boob-tubers treat the Y.P.'s is degrading. Now that the schools are liberated, the next job, it seems to me, is the liberation of the Y.P.'s. That may be a lost cause.

We're going to leave. We have our sights set on Mr. Foreclosure's house at Lake Cachuma. We'll just plan to disappear next Monday night. Found a good hole not far from here. Hope you don't think of us as rats deserting the ship. Keep in touch. You know how.

Up with Worms!
Smudge

There was a dead silence.

Finally, Andromeda spoke up. "I think Smudge has hit the proverbial nail on its proverbial you-know-what."

Skinny pushed his lips forward and wet them. "You plan to leave too?"

"That's it, Skin," said Four Eyes, forcing himself to

look directly into Skinny's eyes. "Things are not much different for us here at Scratchland. Bax and Teresa would love to have our library space for grease racks. The only thing that stops them from pushing us out is that you're our friend."

"All those kids ever think about is cutting down cars and getting to the finish line first!" cried Andromeda. "Ugh!"

"Yeah," said another Worm. "Everything they do is according to their timing equipment. They even eat and sleep for so many thousandths-of-seconds."

"And I don't like the way they boss the Y.P.'s around," added Four Eyes. "Granted the Y.P.'s are pretty limp, but I don't like to see any former kid used as a chamois."

"Whaddya mean, a chamois?"

"Teresa put car wax all over Edwin Crossland's head—told him it was hair tonic!—and made him buff the fenders of her souped-up milk truck. He's had headaches ever since!"

"Bax has over a hundred Y.P.'s just washing cars and picking pebbles out of tires!" exclaimed Andromeda. Her headband shook with anger.

Skinny bit a piece of skin from his index finger and spat it out.

"Where will you go?" he asked in a low voice.

Four Eyes cleared his throat. "There's a place under the Dunphy sisters' basement we can use. They said it was okay."

Then Skinny saw the backpacks of books piled high behind the furnace. The Worms rose, silently picked them up, and belted them on their backs.

A few minutes later, Skinny stood at the rear entrance to the boiler room watching the Worms go off into the night. The noise of the drag strip was muffled by a strong wind, but the smell of exhaust fumes was pungent and brought water to his eyes.

Four Eyes was the last to go. He held out a hand. Skinny took it.

20

A Pledge

Big Alice and Rudy had chased each other in and out among the trees, dunked themselves in the lake, and gorged themselves on berries from a blackberry bush beside Rudy's cave. As the day waned, Big Alice became more and more drawn into herself. After picking burrs out of Rudy's coat, she abruptly sighed and stretched out on a rock. When Rudy nuzzled her, she pushed him away.

"I gotta think," she said.

No more kids. No more tee-jurs, Rudy said, resting his head on his front paws, gazing at Big Alice.

Big Alice stretched, scratched herself, closed her eyes, and slept.

The sun went down, and she was cold. It was dark. Big Alice trembled. She was alone. She got up and moved until she stood under the oldest tree in the preserve. Its trunk measured over forty feet in circumference. There wasn't an animal in the preserve which did not hold it in awe. As Big Alice leaned tremulously against the trunk, a current passed from the tree into herself. Strength swam from the bark into Big Alice's hands as she started to climb the tree. Her feet found knobby toeholds. The energy flow never stopped, but guided Big Alice's hands and feet to ever higher places to grasp, to rest, to push against.

At Scratchland, Skinny climbed the fire escape to the school roof. He saw the colored lights of the drag strip. He heard the cries and curses of the pit crews. The wind grew stronger and drowned out everything but itself. It pushed Skinny's hair and raised goosebumps on his arms. He closed his eyes and drank in the cold air. He placed his hand in his pocket and took out the frosted-glass rabbit. He swiveled it between his thumb and forefinger.

The rabbit spoke with Ida's voice. "Look, Skinny, look out there."

Skinny gazed out over the roof, and in the distance, but strangely clear, he saw a great tree. He saw Big Alice climbing in its branches, halfway up. She clutched at a branch and rested. Then she pulled herself up again.

The tree was a living ladder. In and out of the branches Big Alice swung, higher and higher. Then she stopped again. "I can't! I can't anymore!" she groaned.

"Yes you can, Big Alice. You're almost there," said Skinny. "Keep climbing." He felt that if he reached out he could touch her.

Big Alice climbed until at last she stood among the topmost branches, half fainting, sweat gleaming on her face.

The branches turned transparent beneath her, and Big Alice looked down. Far below at the base of the giant tree were wolves and foxes, antelopes and big-horns, lemmings and deer and bears, armadillos, sloths and waterbucks, wildcats, beavers, toads, hares, and marmosets, all the large and small creatures of untamed places. There were hundreds of them, not one disturbing its neighbor. In the branches of the tree perched birds, every conceivable kind of bird, and they did not make a sound.

Hugging the tree's trunk, Big Alice raised an arm. The creatures stirred as though something wordless passed from her to them. Then, as Skinny watched, Big Alice climbed down until she reached the last branching arms of the tree. They tipped her tenderly onto the ground, and there she fell asleep beside Rudy.

Skinny shivered. He stared at Ida's rabbit in his palm. Then he heard Ida's voice.

"You'll find your own way, you Skinny Malinky. I know you will."

STANLEY KIESEL is a teacher who looks at his chosen career with affection, clarity and humor. He is a poet-in-residence for the Minneapolis public schools and taught kindergarten there and in Los Angeles for twenty years. He has written a book of poems, *The Pearl Is a Hardened Sinner,* and with his wife has raised two well-educated daughters.

The War Between the Pitiful Teachers and the Splendid Kids is a highly original work of Stanley Kiesel's imagination. His favorite book is *Pinocchio.*